VOICES IN THE TREES

NW
813.01
V01
1. Washington (State) — Fiction

© 1989 by   Evergreen Publishing Company, Inc.
200 W. Thomas
Seattle, WA 98119

Library of Congress Catalog Number 89-81326
ISBN 0-937627-08-9

Washington Magazine has produced this book as part of its celebration of Washington's Centennial.

Cover & Book Design by Z Group
Illustrations by Debbie Hanley-McDowell
Calligraphy by Georgia Deaver
Typesetting by Carol Lynn Dillon/The Dillon Group
Printed and bound in USA by Consolidated Press, Berkeley, CA

. . . .

This book is dedicated to

all the writers in Washington
and all the readers they inspire.

it is also
for my father

• •

VOICES IN THE TREES WOULD NOT EXIST WITHOUT THE hearts, hands and minds of many people.

I'd like to thank Mr. Robert D. Best, President of *Washington* magazine, for his vision (and for making it possible for me to begin to realize my own); Amy Tech, business manager/project liaison/solver of problems/good friend; Paul McCollough, Marcus Drake, Keith Askenasi, John Zimmerman & Karen Gutowsky & Z Group for their professional gifts as well as their friendship and support.

Thanks, too, to the staff of *Washington* magazine, to Ed Williams, Diane Carlson and Lisa Hall for their input, and to Tony Tierney, who knew it would all work out right.

TABLE OF CONTENTS

TABLE OF CONTENTS

THAT STATISTIC THAT YOU STUMBLE OVER EVERY SO OFTEN about Washington having the most readers of any state in the country has intrigued me for a very long time. It was the impetus behind this book; if we have the most *readers*, what are the *writers* in Washington up to?

The direct result is in your hand.

There are a LOT of people writing stories, essays, plays, novels, poetry, and non-fiction here at home. I know; over the last few months I've had a rare glimpse into the minds of writers from all over the state.

And I've got to tell you, there's some great stuff out there, coming hard and fast from some incredibly talented people, from all walks of life.

Don't be alarmed if you don't recognize their names. My considered opinion is that you'll be seeing more and more of them.

Just remember you saw them here *first*.

I wanted to print a dozen more stories; so many were worth your time. Since I couldn't give them ALL to you, I've chosen the ones that I believe will touch you, make you laugh, get your attention, cause you to think.

There's a little bit of everything in here: drama, humor, new wave, stream of consciousness, irony. Just like life.

This, then, is the Centennial Edition of THE WASHINGTON ANTHOLOGY. Curl up with a cup of something hot and treat yourself to some of the stories that Washington writers are telling.

(And while you're doing *that*, WE'LL be working on THE WASHINGTON ANTHOLOGY 1990...)

Lisa Tierney
Jasmine Press
October 1989

GHOST DANCER

BY MEGAN BREEN

WENONAH CLAIMED TO BE THE GREAT-GREAT GRAND-daughter of Wovoka, the Paiute Indian prophet and messiah of the Ghost Dance religion. She believed her Indian blood, paled to a fraction, allowed her a heritage favored by spirits and nature. Wenonah was a large woman, tall and heavy. When I was a child, she wore tent dresses to shroud her corpulence and even in later years, having withered to half of what she was, still wore them. Her long, brown hair she knotted at the nape of her neck. Soft, uncooperative wisps framed her face, refusing to lie flat against her head. As I grew older and more vulnerable to the judgements of other children, I felt shame that this overzealous lover of nature and human spirit was my mother.

It was 1963—a year of death, disorder and social statement. It was also the year I turned fourteen, when my shame and pity for Wenonah convoluted itself into something that would gnaw at me for years.

Wenonah and I lived in a small house on the south hill in Spokane. She inherited the two-story white Cape Cod from her mother, along with enough money in trust so the two of us could live comfortably if we were careful. I have only the vaguest childhood recollection of a man as husband and father in that house. He was gone long before he could matter.

In a way, my mother was her own religion. Her abundant belief in herself ripened into faith. But our neighbors didn't see her in the same sacred light. To them she was the eccentric who spent her time absorbed in study; who seldom cleaned her house; and who grew fennel, ginger, Indian turnips and pennyroyal in her yard instead of roses and dahlias. She was the woman who spent hours at Syringa Pond. They thought it most odd that she actually walked into the water. It was not unusual to see Wenonah, knee-deep in the pond, the hem of her dress tucked into the elastic leg bands of her panties, causing the fabric to blouse over. Whether obtaining vegetation with her weed grapple or coming to the aid of injured waterfowl, Wenonah exposed her voluminous thighs shiny and slick from the unctuous waters.

It was her pantheon; she made her pilgrimage to the pond, a neglected piece of city property surrounded by modest homes, almost every day. The neighbors saw it as an eyesore, a blight on the area. But it was Wenonah's safe port, her lover, her family and ultimately her battlefield.

As it was her world, it was my schoolroom. It was there I toddled around learning my colors from the red worm that squirmed along the slime bottom to the iridescent green head of the mallard drake to the soft purple wings of the large, stout dragonfly.

"Today we'll take a close look at the eight downy yellow ducklings," Wenonah announced at breakfast the morning of my fourteenth birthday.

I protested, "This is my birthday. Can't we do something besides go to the pond? Anything."

"Of course we can, Ivy. But this morning let's walk to the pond together. Afterwards you can join your school friends at the bus stop."

I couldn't abide Wenonah walking me to the bus stop. On that morning of all mornings, the last thing I wanted to hear was behind-the-back talk about Ivy Trueman's crazy mother.

"You go ahead, Wenonah. I've got a few more math problems to finish before I leave." I gulped down my milk and headed to the living room and the stack of schoolbooks nestled among Wenonah's journals and jars and jugs set up as pond habitats on the coffee table. My math book wasn't in the stack. "I mean I need to write a few more sentences for my English essay," I yelled back to her. I sat down, opened my *Werriner's*, pulled out some paper and a pen and started to write some nonsense.

Wenonah rummaged in the kitchen, readying her bag of "pond paraphernalia," as she called it. The bag was a many-times-mended rucksack filled with sample bottles, a sketch and note pad, binoculars, scissors and numerous small but essential items for her study.

"All right," she said, not detecting the lie. "I'll head over. If you hurry, you can still get a look before the bus comes."

Off she went in a too-bright pink cotton dress, a knitted shawl draped over one shoulder and the bag of supplies tucked under her arm. I wanted to deny that there could be any link between the sloven woman who sauntered toward Syringa Pond with a gentle sense of purpose, and me, the teenaged girl desperate for acceptance and identity beyond the pond.

I waited until the last possible minute to leave the house, timing it so I might have the dubious pleasure of walking with Sandra Ellison, the singularly most popular girl in the eighth grade. I tried to copy Sandra, the way she dressed and talked and viewed the world. I was dismally unsuccessful.

"So, Ivy," Sandra said, "Today is your birthday."

"Please don't tell anybody," I pleaded, knowing that was the surest of all ways to get the word out.

"What did you get for your birthday? I got a little transistor radio for mine. It's real cute," she said. "I can stick it in my purse or tuck it in my pocket. What did your mom get you?"

If I could lie to Wenonah about my homework, I could lie to Sandra about a birthday present. "I got a cashmere sweater."

"Wow!" Sandra looked at me for the first time since we started walking that morning. "My mother says I'm too young for cashmere. How come you aren't wearing it? Seems like the perfect day to have it on."

I stammered, "It's kind of fancy for school."

"Sure," Sandra smiled at me, "sure it is. I'd have thought your mom would get you a frog net or some pond scum to look at under the microscope." She laughed and stepped out in front of me.

The bus collected neighborhood kids on the corner of Syringa Road and Maple Street, at the easternmost corner of the pond. A group of ten gathered there every morning. Sandra, who always managed to arrive a comfortable distance ahead of me, stood with the other kids at the corner.

As I approached, I looked quickly to see if Wenonah was in sight. If she was nest-watching, she'd be hunkered down some distance from the water's edge, hopefully hidden in the reed grass and cattails bordering the pond. I didn't see her; she was camouflaged from the ducks and from my schoolmates.

Just as the school bus groaned to a stop in front of us, Wenonah emerged from a cluster of tall grasses and yelled, "Ivy, there are nine, not eight, ducklings!" She waved her binoculars at me, catching the strap in her hair. As the other kids boarded the bus, they started mocking Wenonah with sneers, laughter and duck calls. Taunts of roast duck for dinner, the appearance of the Swamp Thing, and Midnight-at-the-Pond Perfume ricocheted around me. I looked away from Syringa Pond as the bus pulled away, wishing she'd fall in and drown, her body swallowed up by the ooze.

That morning on the bus I took a vow of eternal silence toward Wenonah. I broke the vow that very afternoon as I opened the back screen door.

She was sitting at the kitchen table, not reading or studying as was the normal occurrence at that hour. She was sitting with her hands folded on the table in front of her. In the center of the table sat a package, awkwardly wrapped with last year's Christmas paper and tied with a string of frayed red yarn.

"Sorry I didn't have any birthday wrap."

"What is it?" I asked.

Wenonah leaned toward me and whispered, "I don't know. Why don't we sit around all evening and guess?"

"Nah. Let's open it instead," I said, ripping the hundreds of tiny red and green Santas from the box. Lying in the box was my gift, a navy blue miniskirt and a blue and white striped blouse. "Thanks, Wenonah."

"I ordered it from Sears. If it isn't what you want, we can send it back."

"Never. It's perfect," I told her. We reached across the table to each other and held hands for a moment.

"I'm sorry about this morning with your school friends. I was excited about the ninth duckling," Wenonah said as she rose from the table. "I can make a perfect ass of myself sometimes."

"It's all right, really."

"No, it probably isn't all right. But it won't be a problem much longer." She had a strange tone in her voice, almost defeatist, very unlike her.

"What do you mean?"

"The city is draining the pond," she said flatly, standing at the sink, rinsing lettuce for our salad, the water from the kitchen faucet cascading slowly over it as she broke it apart.

"I don't get it," I told her.

Wenonah sat down again at the table. "Some city engineers were at the pond today. Figuring and taking depth readings. Somebody bought the land from the city and they're going to drain it and build some houses." She stared at her hands, folded once again in front of her, wet with water from the sink. "The entire pond will be sucked up and flushed down the sewer."

Our silence was broken by the realization that the water was still running in the sink. I turned it off. "What are you going to do?" I asked.

She didn't seem to hear me at first. Then she looked at me and said, "We've got some grebes nesting for the first time in years. Three eggs."

I was at a loss for words. It was one of those difficult moments for a child—casting about for the right words to console a parent. "Maybe they don't understand how important the pond is to you?" I finally said.

"Me? Oh, no. It's the pond itself, you see. Eventually, when it's time, it will dry up. But not now, not by sucking the life out of it. I can't let that happen." She paused to take a deep breath and then, as if inspired by the intake of air, announced with assurance, "I'll do something."

Wenonah began her campaign to save the pond the next morning with numerous fruitless phone calls. No one person seemed able to take responsibility for any decision-making in city government. After speaking with the mayor, she was teeming with aggravation.

"Why don't you call Chester Mertens at the high school?" I asked. Chester Mertens was a biology teacher, a frustrated anthropologist, who had to satisfy himself with teaching the life sciences to less than grateful hordes of sophomore boys and girls.

Every year he called upon Wenonah to handle the pond ecology unit. She was a gifted teacher, enchanting students with details about the duckweed, the water striders and whirligig beetles. She twisted into focus the kaleidoscope of different zones of the pond and the micro-cosmic colonies of small drifting animals and plants. Wenonah shared her view of the pond with the students as if she were herself a citizen of its remarkable community. Every fall she became pond poet laureate reciting her ode to the abundance and dependence of life.

"That's an idea," she declared. "But what can he do?" Wenonah paused in thought, shrugged her shoulders and mumbled, "I'll give him a try."

She called him that evening. Yes, he had heard about the pond, and no, he had no idea what she might do. He told her he could probably teach the unit using film.

Preparations for draining the pond went on. Wenonah continued her telephoning. She went as far as a state senator, who was encouraging but not helpful. All the while she watched the city's activity at the pond from a grassy knoll on its west side as if she were a scout sent out to reconnoiter the enemy position and determine the advantage it might have, and the best means of attack.

Two days before the draining was to begin, a monstrous yellow compression engine, mounted on an equally menacing truck, took its position at the edge of the pond, two tremendous tentacular hoses lying at its side. I knew Wenonah, for all her size and strength, was no match for the life-sucking machine.

"I've nothing left to do," she told me. She thumbed through the phone book that evening, writing down numbers as she found them. "The newspapers, radio and television. They need to know."

I had visions of Wenonah making a spectacular show of herself, much worse than stepping out from the cattails and announcing the arrival of a ninth duckling to half of the eighth grade class.

"You can't just call and say somebody's draining the pond, come quick and stop it," I said.

"Of course I can't," she said. "But they'll show up if they're teased a little." At that point I saw a cavalcade of shame descending upon me.

I was awakened the next morning by a siren screaming up the hill. Normally I awoke to Wenonah's early morning sounds rumbling up from the kitchen. But that morning, no bacon sizzled in the pan, no percolator announced another beginning and no newspaper pages snapped and crackled open.

I called down, but there was no answer.

On the kitchen table, next to a clean cereal bowl and a box of Wheaties, was a note. It said the answer had come to her in a vision. Another siren pierced the early morning neighborhood silence. I feared the worst—some sort of Indian sacrifice.

Most children I knew had been lulled to sleep by Mother Goose, Brer Rabbit or Dr. Seuss, but not me. Wenonah told me stories, wonderful stories about the world in its chaotic, rumbling beginning.

She told me about beneficent Indian spirits and feral children endowed with supernatural gifts from their animal caretakers. When I was old enough to understand its importance to her, she told me about Wovoka.

It was he who took the message to the troubled Indian tribes that they must not fight, rather that they should always do right and practice brotherly love. He preached nonviolence toward the white people.

Wovoka taught his followers the Ghost Dance. For four nights they danced. The intensity and fervent action of the dance would ultimately cause the Earth to tremble and create a series of catastrophic events which would end in the entire White race being swallowed up in the quaking Earth.

Only the Indian believers would survive, along with all their dead ancestors brought back to life. They would reenter a world as pure as the beginning, with game roaming free, long, graceful grasses carpeting the plains, an abundant nature untouched.

Wenonah always told that part of the story with a great booming voice, as if in imitation of an angry Earth. Then she'd become solemn again and tell me about the ghost shirts made of cloth and decorated with magic symbols. Some dancers believed the ghost shirts made them invincible. Wovoka knew differently. No one listened to him. And because his warning fell on unhearing ears, some followers fell into misery and death. The Indian Eden would never be.

With vivid images of Wenonah bedecked in a modern-day ghost shirt, I rushed from the house, nearly knocking over Sandra Ellison.

When I arrived at the pond, two police cars, a fire truck and an ambulance were pulled up close to the edge of the pond. Several men with cumbersome cameras slung over their shoulders and pads and pencils in hand stood around one of the police officers. The emergency vehicles obstructed my view of the pond.

I ran by the kids gathered at the bus stop, who wouldn't relinquish their places in line to save their lives, or anyone else's. I kept saying aloud that I hadn't meant I wanted Wenonah to drown. I elbowed my way through the men, desperately hoping my imagination had over-powered my already tentative hold on reality.

In the middle of the pond, sitting in an old rowboat that had been in the garage for twenty years, was Wenonah. My relief that she hadn't drowned or been swallowed by the pond's muck was soon replaced by familiar embarrassment.

She had braided her hair Indian style, two long brown plaits resting on her abundant bosom. Around her head she had tied a headband, decorated with beads and a few duck feathers.

The water was barely three inches from the top of the boat, which was trying to stay afloat with Wenonah and a brown grocery bag as cargo.

A tall, thin man with a fedora pulled low over his forehead asked one of the officers what was going on. He held a note pad in the palm of his hand, pencil poised and ready for the scoop of the week.

The officer looked tired and disgusted. He snapped an answer to the reporter. "We got an anonymous tip there was going to be a rape and murder down here at sunup. Right at the end of my shift, wouldn't you know."

"Yeah," the reporter coaxed him, "So what happened? And who's she?" He pointed toward Wenonah.

"Says she wants people to know what's happening. That they're draining the pond. It doesn't take a genius to see that, now does it?" the officer said, turning away and heading toward his patrol car.

Wenonah raised a makeshift megaphone, fashioned from rolled-up newspapers, to her mouth. Chanting in a strong, confident voice, she began one of the lectures she had given Chester Mertens' sophomores for years.

The reporter hailed Wenonah. "What's your name, Lady?"

"Wenonah Trueman," she yelled. "Trueman with an 'e'."

"What's the story about rape and murder?"

Wenonah shifted her weight in the boat. Those of us standing on the bank gasped, thinking it would empty its passenger into the water. Wenonah managed to steady it; the crowd sighed its relief.

Again Wenonah put her megaphone to her mouth and announced:

"The city and a land developer are ruining this ecosystem. They're going to build three houses here. They're raping this pond, murdering all the plants and animals of its community."

Then she fell into her lecture-chant once more.

With a flick of his wrist, the reporter closed his notebook. "No story here," he said, and walked away.

The small neighborhood crowd which had assembled slowly dispersed amid smiles and laughter. They probably figured it was no big deal, strange Wenonah was at it again.

I made my way to a flowering hemlock and sat next to it. So this had been her vision, I thought. She had seen herself saving what she loved by protesting from a tippy old rowboat in the middle of her world.

She looked ridiculous.

A heavy-set man in a sweat-stained t-shirt and yellow hard hat climbed down from the truck that carried the compressor. He yelled to Wenonah, "You'd better paddle in, lady, or you'll be ass-deep in mud in about twenty-four hours."

Wenonah ignored his warning, saying something about sharing her fate with the crayfish and pickerel. The workman waved her off as just another nuisance and headed for his machine.

The compressor, with its hose in the water, groaned to a start and then pumped in a loud, steady rhythm that echoed off the houses surrounding Syringa Pond. The compressor worked until the noon hour, when the lone crewman took his lunch break. The opposite end of the hose flushed itself out into the street and down a drainage hole.

Wenonah, her brown grocery bag full of food, took lunch when the compressor man did, as if it was a civilized war she waged.

The machine started pumping once again at one o'clock and continued with little interruption throughout the day.

Once in a while the crewman had to stop it and clear away obstructions. I hated to think what they might be. I thought of the grebes and the turtles, especially the one on which I'd painted a silver star when I was five. We named him Matt Dillon and had seen him as recently as three weeks before.

I had to get away from the pond.

At dusk I returned, determined to say something to Wenonah, some words of encouragement. But another group of curious neighbors had gathered, and I found myself once again trying to look inconspicuous beside the hemlock.

Wenonah continued her lecture until this last group of onlookers walked away. I wondered if they realized they were walking away from the pond for the last time.

The sun set and Wenonah remained in the middle of the pond. A full moon that night put her in a ghostly light; the moonlight, playing off her prominent nose and high cheekbones, made her dress look muted and soft against the blackness of the pond.

From my cowardly perch I saw Wenonah for the first time in my life. She floated on a sea of her own belief, and, try as she might to have me out there with her, I didn't belong. I couldn't see or hear or feel what she did. I wondered if anyone truly could.

Her head dropped to her chin. I was afraid she'd tip again, but she was awakened by the voice of a man calling from the bank. "Wenonah. Wenonah, can you hear me?"

"Chester Mertens, is that you?" she called.

I could see Chester now. He moved closer to the edge of the water.

"I'm sorry I couldn't be more help to you, Winnie," he said sadly. "Can I do anything for you now?"

She held on to the sides of the boat to steady it. "Thank you, no. Chester, I'm afraid my protest has turned into a very personal wake of sorts. I'll just sit it out and be gone when it's all over."

"Are you sure?" he asked.

"You can walk by the house for me and check on Ivy. Make sure she's okay."

"I'd be happy to. Good night, Winnie." He started away from the pond, heading directly for the hemlock. I stepped out from behind it and stood in his path. Neither of us spoke. He tipped his hat and walked past me.

I settled back down again, drowsy and aching. I pulled my sweater close and thought as I drifted off that Chester Mertens called my mother "Winnie," the closest to a term of endearment I ever heard for her.

During the night, I had the dream that even now continues to disturb my sleep. Wenonah is in the middle of a great stadium. The towns-people and the schoolchildren are all crammed in the stands yelling and jeering at her. She is wearing a fringed buckskin dress—she's beautiful with a mystical, radiant light surrounding her. The people start throwing things at her—rocks and dead frogs and turtle shells marked with silver stars. Everything strikes her and she begins to bleed. I sit and watch it all happen. I want to get up and go help her, but I can't move. I'm cemented to the seat; my feet weigh a ton. I scream at her to dance, to do the Ghost Dance to make us all disappear and restore the world to what it was. She finally hears me and begins dancing. Her move-ments are fluid and sensual. I feel such pride in her. Her movements become frenetic and finally she becomes a spiraling mass of blue, green, purple and red light. She disappears.

I awoke to the blinding light of a new sun. It was a dream. Wenonah was in place in the pond, her boat had shifted somewhat and she now faced east.

I walked home and sat at the kitchen table, weary from the long night. I filled the bowl Wenonah had left for me with Wheaties and looked through the morning paper. Nothing about Wenonah Trueman, Trueman with an "e".

The compressor started again at eight o'clock and it banged away all day. No stop for lunch this time. At dusk there was silence; it was finished.

I wanted to go to the pond, or what was left of it, and help Wenonah get home. I couldn't.

I brewed some herb tea and made toast so she could eat when she got home. I watched for her a long time at the front window.

Finally she came. She was caked with mud to her waist; her feet made odd squishing sounds as she walked.

"Wenonah, are you okay?" I asked, putting my arm around her the best I could.

"Tired, mostly," she said, "And just a little dirty, don't you think?"

"You smell kind of ripe, too."

She laughed. "More than kind of."

Wenonah hosed the mud off in the back yard and went up for a shower. I set out her tea and made some fresh toast with apple butter.

She came down still looking tired, but refreshed and smiling as if she'd won her battle. She sat at the table and said, "What a perfect meal. Just what I wanted. Thank you, Ivy."

That night we sat on the back porch and Wenonah told me again about Wovoka and his mission. She talked about his vision of God instructing him to teach his people the dance ritual.

"Did you see God last night?" I asked her.

"I saw only you," she said.

Wenonah died two years ago in April. Bedridden with diabetes and nearly blind, she could only watch her world as she remembered it. She tried to read and reread her copious notes taken over the years at the pond until the last pencil-thin threads of sight faded.

Last spring, Chester Mertens, himself in poor health, succeeded in having a small drinking fountain dedicated to Wenonah in Syringa Park.

The houses were never built. The builder went bankrupt and the good citizens decided the empty lot would be a perfect place for a park.

I flew in from New York for the dedication, my first time back since Wenonah died.

Chester and the maintenance man, a few curious children and I stood around a waist-high cement fountain. Chester had a plaque made with Wenonah's name, her birth and death dates and the title *Naturalist* after her name.

He said a few words about Wenonah and her contribution to environmental education as I watched a handsome fisher spider spin a net for her young on the pedestal of the fountain.

ONE IF BY MAGIC

BY M. ELAYN HARVEY

THIS WAS THE PORTENTOUS MOMENT: MRS. LILLIAN McKean leaning out her front door, in her pink house dress with the white daisies and her pink slippers, waiting for the mailman. It was foggy and January this morning, but she was hardly aware of the misting cold, or of the gray tabby bounding into the house past her feet, or even of the mailman; only the packet in his hand held any importance. The bundle was wrapped in magazines and secured with a rubber band. As it came onto the porch, came into her outstretched hand, she smiled, warmed inside by the renewed infusion of serene anticipation this moment always bestowed.

The mailman touched his cap. "Morning, Mrs. McKean."

"Morning. Lovely morning," she replied hastily, wanting to close the door, now that she had her mail.

"Prit near to snow, I'd say. Gettin' on all right, are you, what with the Mister gone?"

"Yes, fine. Fine."

"Lewis, down the block, is havin' a garage sale."

"Yes, I know."

He touched his cap again, and turned away to resume his route.

Lillian shut the door on pleasantries already forgotten, and carried her mail through the parlor, a room with sagging, blanket-draped furniture huddling a cold woodstove, a room between the front door and her kitchen, where she lived. She set the bundle on the drab formica table and pulled out her lone chair, a sorry thing, the seat patched with duct tape. The neglect was invisible to her, by reason of long association and the anticipation that was most delicious just now; she had glimpsed a long manila envelope inside the colorful magazine wrapping. She itched to take it up and open it, but first there were rituals to perform.

Not that she was consciously aware of that fact, or of its origin. It was such an old superstition, so well lived in it was never questioned. Before indulging in any good activity (such as the opening of presents on Christmas morn), her father, and Mister McKean after him, had insisted that perfect order must be accomplished in one's surroundings: breakfast dishes washed, tables dusted, floors swept, pet fed. Only then, when all one's effort had somehow put the moment right, could one set about accepting a reward with a sure faith that now it was deserved.

Lillian washed and dusted and swept, her mind never once leaving the packet on the table. She didn't care for housework; the ritual was intended to secure that faithful rightness, which was to her an objective more real than the religious woman's hope of heaven. For wasn't she always receiving in bounteous proportions for her effort? Why, "prit near" every morning the U.S. Postal Service delivered the seeds, and one day she would reap a harvest of luxury. She winked at Pippin and filled his cat dish.

Which sweepstakes envelope might it be? Publisher's Market Grand? Magazine Bonanza? Digest Bonus Warehouse? Not the Grand; that was last week. She had been selected as a finalist for the five million dollar super prize. This category had also entitled her to a Tudor mansion with an English garden, or two point five million dollars in cash; a cedar chalet to be built at her favorite winter vacation site, or half a million in cash; or an around-the-world cruise, or if she preferred, fifty thousand dollars. Her life was continually teetering on the brink of wealth. It wouldn't be long now.

"Yes, Pippin, something'll happen soon, I can feel it. You'll get cooked giblets at every meal, an' a silk pillow afterwards for your washin' and nappin'. You just wait an' see."

She put the kettle on the boil for her tea, then arranged her work things beside the mail: letter opener, scissors, pen, postage stamps, and her little spiral-bound book, in which she recorded numbers and addresses. These things were placed in their imagined order, like sacramentals on an altar. She carried her steaming mug, with its trailing tea-bag string, to the table and made herself comfortable.

Now was the time.

But she was not to be hasty; this penultimate moment must be given its due. This was the rooftop of her day, and from its rarefied perspective a future of seven-digit bank accounts spread down before her with an inner certainty stronger than hope. Soon she would be that most magical of ladies: a rich woman. Why, she would never have to worry about meeting monthly bills. She could buy anything she fancied; do anything; go anywhere she liked dressed in fur coats and real pearls, and smelling of perfume and powder like the fine ladies in church, a vision so real she felt it to be prophetic. It was only a matter of time. With this joy firmly in hand, she opened her mail.

There was ritual in this, too. The best was saved for last. She pulled off the rubber band and separated the magazines. These she took into the late Mister's den. The small room was unheated and bare of furniture; she had sold the desk, filing cabinet, and his dusty books last winter to pay the heating bill. The room was no longer a den, no longer held any souvenir of Old Man McKean. Not that she was unkind in her memories of him. He had lived a good life on her casseroles and optimism, but he'd had no ambition to better his station or hers. He had puttered the summers in his backyard garden, and his winters in the den, doing accounts and reading *Poor Richard's Almanac* and Zane Grey westerns. He had been a tolerant man, but no dreamer, unless one counted adventures of the old west.

So there was nothing on the bookshelves and bare floorboards but stack upon stack of unopened magazines: three years' worth. She added the new ones to the nearest pile and returned to the kitchen.

She sat down again, pinched the inside corners of her eyes, and squinted up at the harsh dish light on the ceiling. Despite her economical use of forty-watt bulbs, it glared. She sighed and laid apart the renewals for three more magazines. She didn't look at them; never reading, she never renewed. But that didn't mean the magazines were unwanted. The rightness which she applied to her preliminaries she also applied to the act of entering sweepstakes.

If any entry offered four magazines at a reduced cover price, and the option for three low monthly installments (and they could not imagine anyone saying no to such an offer, when it included a full refund), then she could not deprive herself of the opportunity. Not the opportunity of accepting the magazines; the opportunity not to deprive herself of the chance to put everything right. Every magazine stamp box must be filled, the super prize circle must be covered with its gold-foil seal, the lucky numbers card must be clipped and folded on its dashed lines. If all was not right, the prize selection department might think her not worthy to participate in their sweepstakes, and more importantly, might not be inclined to award her the prize. So, she always ordered magazines.

She also set aside the city utility bill and came, at last, to the envelope. It was from Digest Bonus Warehouse, and in the window was a replica of the grand-prize-winning check made out to Mrs. L. McKean for the amount of Six Million, Two Hundred and Fifty Thousand Dollars.

"My, oh my." She read it again. One hundred and sixty-seven thousand dollars a year for the rest of her life.

"Oh my!" The sooner she mailed her entry, the more she could win, and a special courier would arrive at her door within fourteen days with her first check. Reply on or before: January twenty-first. She had a full two weeks, but this would be out in the afternoon mail; she was always as prompt as possible.

Carefully, she slit open the entry and spread the forms and game cards, checks and magazine stamp sheets. She clipped the perforations, signed the validations, folded the dashes, and pasted the stamps and squares and circles on their proper places. Not too much moisture on the tongue lest the paper fall off. There was a bonus prize card filled with five little silver circles: The Lucky Derby game. She must select the winning horse to be eligible for a one-week London vacation or five thousand in cash. This was tricky. The officials expected her to pick the right one. She studied the names. "Golden Bugle" was the only one that sounded lucky. She held her breath and scratched off the silver with her letter opener. It said, *win*.

Oh, how wonderful — how incredible! She, Mrs. Lillian McKean, had chosen the only circle marked *win!* Surely, this was a sign. She endorsed the back and slipped it, with the rest of the entry, into the return *Yes, I am ordering* envelope. She recorded her lucky numbers in her spiral book, and the addresses to receive the list of winners. She checked the contents to be certain all was right, sealed it shut, and attached a stamp.

Only then did she sit back, drink her tepid tea, and bask in the pleasure of a job well done. An entry well worth the prize-winning check, which would soon arrive at her front door.

Thinking of the door put her in mind of the Lewis' garage sale. It was only eleven; there might be something left to browse through. No telling what one was apt to find one could not do without. She would mail the sweepstakes entry on her way.

It did indeed look like it was getting ready to snow. The grayish-white clouds had closed in, pushing the fog to crawl along Carrol Street and wreath the houses across the way in bluish mist. The air had that sharp scent of snow in it, and the sidewalks felt slick.

Mrs. McKean walked slowly, turning up the collar of her navy coat against the icy cold. She tightened her red scarf. There was no traffic. She had the distinct feeling she was quite alone in the winter world. This made her feel all the more unique and favored. When she came to the mailbox, she dropped in her entry and continued down the block; now stepping a bit more confidently with a trust that one day soon she would be bidding good riddance to this shabby, narrow street with its cracked sidewalks and aging houses.

Lillian approached the end of the block and Ed Lewis' neat clapboard saltbox where he lived with his son, his son's wife and their two girls. She knew something of the old man from Mister McKean. They used to garden together, exchanging the merits of red potatoes over Idaho, and whether pole beans or bush were easier to till. These had been merely matters of preference, and many an evening found them sitting amiably in the back yard, drinking imported ale and talking of the Civil War, a subject which they could readily commiserate upon, having both had ancestors in the Confederacy. In fact, if old Ed were to be believed, he was related to Robert E. Lee by marriage. Often she'd heard him say to the Mister how if the South had won, he should now be a rich man.

Well, it hadn't and he wasn't. Couldn't even afford to have the driveway paved; and the garage was set back and separate from the house, so that she had to make her way along the high, uneven center to avoid the frozen mud puddles.

As she gained the dry garage and wiped her shoes, it began to snow. She would have a cursory look around, now that she was here, and hurry back before it got too deep. The garage was a double-wide, and free of cars for the time being, as both the younger Lewis and his wife worked out of town. The cement was cluttered with boxes of knickknacks and discarded small appliances, assorted rusty tools and horseshoes. There were bedsteads with wire springs and a rack of women's clothing; she recalled that Mr. Lewis was a widower.

In the back was a roomy workshop, heated nicely by a small wood stove. From among the benches and sawhorses came the old man himself to greet her. He was plank thin and not overly tall, so he didn't tower over her, a tendency in men which she didn't like. The Mister had been of medium height, and that was what had first attracted her.

Ed's chin was clean-shaven, but he had an unruly mustache and eyebrows, both peppery and making a bristly muff around his seal-blue eyes. Fate had given him the kindly look of a character out of Dr. Seuss. He wore faded bib overalls, a corduroy jacket, and a slouchy tweed hat. This he doffed to reveal a small balding dome surrounded by a gray forest.

"Good day, Mrs. McKean. Out and about, eh? An' I see it's a-snowin'. Well, been expecting it all day. If it's gonna snow, might well as do it an' get it over. An' how are you?"

"Just fine. I was at the mailbox an' thought, since I was that far, I would come see what you have."

He nodded at this, smiling. "Lookin' for anythin' particular?"

She glanced around. "Oh, you know how it is. You never know what you lack, 'til you see it somewheres else."

"Aye, that's the truth. How's your Pippin?"

"Oh, fine. Why, what's this?" She stooped and brought up an old lamp from a box at her feet. It was small and, judging by the weight, made of brass, though now a tarnished green-brown. It had a bulb but no shade. Its cord hugged its slender base in frayed coils.

"Don't know if it works. Belonged to my dad. The shade's around here somewheres." He eyed the boxes and brought up a rumpled wad of newsprint, which he unrumpled.

"Why, it's Tiffany," exclaimed Mrs. McKean, when she saw it. "I haven't seen the like in forty years or better. You'll not be wantin' to part with that too cheap."

"Well, can't say what I'd be wantin'. Folks nowadays see it's past its time. They want somethin' a might stronger to read by, though my dad swore it was the best to see clear on." He took the lamp from her and retreated to the workshop. "Let's have a look-see."

She followed and warmed her hands over the stove while Ed set the lamp on his bench, adjusted the shade and plugged it in.

"Fancy that, the bulb's still sound. I 'member my dad bendin' on his financial page every night, an' mutterin' how the light could sure pick up them stocks. Didn't look like nothin' but 'rithmetic done in letters to me. He never lost a cent, though. Had a good eye for the game, he did. Got out before the Crash." He stood back. "Makes a nice glow, don't it?"

Mrs. McKean saw that it did lay down a gentle light, gilding the clean carpenter bench, and above it the planes and rasps and saws on the pegboard wall. The jewel red and gold of the Tiffany shade gave off a cozy radiance, and made her recall younger days: quiet evenings sitting with the Mister in their humble parlor, him reading and her knitting, and the wood stove so warm between them, they didn't give a mind to winter outside. She realized she had been happier then. The thought irritated her with a strange impatience. She cast her eye on the snow, which was turning the ground white at an alarming pace.

"I could use a good reading lamp," she said, remembering the kitchen glare. "How much?"

"Well, since it's you askin', the widow of a friend an' all. An' seein' as how the shade ain't broke — say, three dollars?"

"Quite reasonable." She opened her purse and gave him three bills.

These he put inside a worn cigar box. He unplugged the lamp and placed it in her hands, then escorted her to the garage door.

"Looks mighty slippery out there. I'm thinkin' you'll need a steady hand to help you home."

"Oh, I wouldn't want to be a bother. Why, who would mind your sale? Really, it isn't but up the block."

Yet, as she was in the midst of this protest, he had put on his hat, taken her elbow, and began guiding her down the snowy drive.

"I reckon this late, anyone was to come, they already did. If you please, I can't abide a worry of you fallin' and gettin' hurt, an' lyin' in the cold with not another body about."

"You're very kind, Mister Lewis."

He glanced at her with amusing surprise. "As much for my peace o' mind." His breath came out like the steam from her dryer vent. "An' a lady ought not to be made familiar with such weather," he added. "She could catch her death. How's your woodshed?"

They had turned onto the sidewalk. "Oh, I can't take the bother of splittin' and packin'. It's easier to close off half the house, an' let the furnace do my work."

"Aye, but there's nothin' like a toasty fire to drive the chill off the ol' bones." And here he nearly said more, but perhaps thinking better of it, was silent.

They passed the mailbox again, and Mrs. McKean thought of her entry. When she had first dropped it in, she pictured it already in the hands of benefactors, and a miracle on its way to her. But now, as she imagined it lying alone in the dark, waiting for the mail truck, it seemed a lonely thing to pin one's hopes upon. Stubbornly, she put the thought from her mind. She had worked too long to admit she might be faltering in her faith. Three years of dedication had to count for something.

"Here you go." Ed was leading her up to the porch of her house. "A little silver paste on that lamp'll shine it up real fine. I woulda done it, you see, but I didn't think to be sellin' it."

She turned to him. "If you'd rather not . . . ?"

"No, I'd be pleased if you had it. I meant I don't hardly ever sell a thing, an' that suits me. But see, my boy gets to yappin' about all my junk, so I set it out an' put up a sign. In a few days I put it all away again, an' he's hushed down for a while. Got to keep the peace." He shifted his hat respectfully. "Good day, Mrs. McKean."

"Good day, and thank you." She brushed the snow from her coat, shook out her scarf, and went in to find her silver polish.

The lamp hardly looked the same; its base now had a fine patina, almost like old gold. She had washed and buffed the shade until it gleamed. But, sitting in its soft light on her kitchen table, something didn't look right. It came to her that a nice tablecloth might be an improvement. So she ironed her best ivory linen and spread it out. Yes, much better. Only now, the window sheers beyond the table looked limp. She washed and ironed them, and cleaned the window.

When she had rehung the curtains, she stepped back and admired the marvelous change. Except —

That chair would not do. She took it to the laundry room; and from her bedroom, she brought out the Chippendale that had come from her mother's estate. She rubbed it with paste wax until it shone, and set it at the table. Why, this could be a rich woman's dining room! Except —

The china hutch; she hadn't noticed how dull it had become, and the glass was filmed. She set to work with an eager delight, already imagining how wonderful it would look.

Thus passed her day. And that evening, she sat in the Chippendale, with the linen on her knees, and ate her simple meal on a setting of her English Rose she had kept stored in the hutch all these years. It sparkled under the light of the Tiffany lamp, and she basked in a warm, happy awe at the fine things she had forgotten she owned. For once she enjoyed her scrambled eggs, toast, and marmalade. This plain pekoe was a delicacy in her fragile flower cup. Lillian went to bed that night with a rare smile of satisfaction.

The Tiffany lamp spread a warm glow on the morning table. Lillian sat at her breakfast tea, in a black wool dress, stockings, and two sweaters; there was a chill in the house from the foot of snow outside her window. She lingered, admiring the stained-glass lamp shade and planning her day; thinking specifically how the Persian rug in the bedroom should look much better laid here to cover the cold linoleum. It saw little use back there, and its colors matched the reds and golds of the shade so nicely. Yes, she would move it. And wasn't there a picture in the attic? The one by Monet; a girl with red hair. It would look perfect on the far wall. She remembered, now, that she had put it away after the Mister died, quite unexpectedly in his sleep, at the untimely age of fifty-two. It had been his favorite picture because, he said, it reminded him of her when she was young. Her loss of him had been so jarring that she had taken it down, and put away the things they had used together. Now, she should like to see it again, to remember less lonely times.

As she mused, the doorbell rang. She opened the door to see a smile of relief on the mailman's face.

He handed her the mail. "I was afraid you'd taken to bed ill."

"My, no, Mister Parish. I'm quite well, thank you."

"Good to see you lookin' so fine. Morning." He touched his cap and left, smiling still.

She shut the door and took her mail to the kitchen. When she had laid it on the table, she stood looking down at the magazines secured with the inevitable rubber band, and there was a strange wondering in her mind of why it looked so different this morning. She sat down, pulled off the band, and laid everything flat. The same mail: two magazines, three subscription bills, one renewal, the electric bill, a congressional pamphlet, and a sweepstakes bulletin from Magazine Bonanza. Her eyes fixed on the amount offered: ten million dollars.

Ten Million Dollars? Some of her old excitement returned. She had never seen so large a grand prize! Quickly, she took her letter opener and other things from the hutch drawer and laid them out. She slit open the envelope and skimmed the pages.

There were four entry cards, but the special offer was limited: only two magazines per entrant. Besides the grand prize, she was, as a valued customer, guaranteed to win either five million, two and a half million, one million, or a bonanza of other exciting prizes: houses, cars, boats, trips, entertainment centers . . . no obligation . . . enter today: "You could be our next lucky multi-millionaire."

For some reason she couldn't explain, this did not impress her. Where on earth could she keep a boat? Her carport was hardly big enough to cover her little Volvo.

She spread the sheet of magazine stamps and studied it under the lamp. Why, the prices for some of these were almost sixty dollars a year. She hadn't noticed that before. She calculated in her head how many magazines she had purchased in the last three years. There were four major publishers which sent sweepstakes announcements. They mailed about every six weeks (or nine times a year). They offered, on the average, three magazines per entry. The average price of which was twenty dollars; that was . . . My goodness, that was over six hundred dollars! Why, if she had that six hundred dollars right now, she wouldn't be worrying about heating bills.

The bonus game card caught her eye. There were twelve silver shamrocks. If she could uncover the three (and only three) which said *win*, she could be eligible for an extra fifty thousand dollars in cash. If more than three shamrocks were scratched off, the game was void. The card looked odd. She peered at it closely; then held it up between her eyes and the light. What she saw shocked and betrayed her. Why, she could see through the silver. And they *ALL* said *win*.

There was no game. No skill or luck was required. No rightness was necessary. She looked at the stamps again. Their multitude pressed on her mind a thought she'd never considered until now. All these magazines, and all these mailings; it dawned on her. The prize award committee was not an altruistic benefactor granting huge sums of money; they were a business. And their business was selling magazines. How could she have been so blind?

She sat for long moments thinking nothing coherent, feeling only a grave, worldly disappointment. Then she smirked, and gave a little laugh and shook her head. She repeated an old adage learned from her mother.

"Fool me once, shame on you; fool me twice, shame on me."

Deliberately, she folded up the pages and laid them aside, along with the renewal. She opened the subscription bills, and wrote across each one, in very serious capitals: CANCEL.

As Lillian pressed the last envelope, she was distracted by a thumping on her front porch. It couldn't be the cat; Pippin was sleeping in the bedroom. By the time she'd risen and opened the door, no one was in sight. But there at her feet lay a bundle of kindling and a tote of split wood.

"Now, who . . . ?" But she knew who had performed this unexpected kindness; how he had spoken yesterday of woodsheds and warm fires.

"Why, bless his heart."

She brought them in and quickly shut the door. A fire would be very welcome; with the snow she had felt chilled all day. Yes, a nice toasty fire; and she had just the paper with which to start one. She brought the entry forms and magazines from the table, tore and crumpled them, and laid the makings.

When she had touched the match, and the wood had caught, and the smoke drafted neatly up the chimney, she smiled. The warmth seeped lazily into her bones and the smell of hot cast iron brought back her girlhood on the farm. In the mornings, her first sight had been of her mother stoking the big cookstove in the kitchen. She recalled how every other day the house was spiced with the mouth-watering aroma of fresh baked bread.

My, how long since she had baked her own loaves, and when had she stopped? When and why had she put aside her knitting? How long since she had done up her own batch of orange marmalade? These little personal accomplishments had given her such pleasure. How could she have forgotten?

She shut the stove door, turned down the damper, and stood warming her hands. The heat felt so good she began to feel warm inside, too, eager to take up past enjoyments that had given her their own simple rightness. She would bake bread today. And yes, take a fresh loaf over to Ed Lewis, to thank him for the wood.

IN THE MIST

BY REBECCA D. WILKINSON NICKELL

THE HUM OF THE MOTOR BREAKS THROUGH THE PATTER of the rain. As my small Fiat glides to a halt, droplets gently drum an erratic rhythm on the roof; sheets of water glaze the windshield. Between the boards that make up the ramshackle fence, I look down the hill to the arena.

It doesn't look like I'll be doing much riding today. The worn dirt track has been transformed into an oval puddle, water welling up in the hoof prints Kismet and I made yesterday during our daily exercise. The spring drizzle caresses my face and hands, quietly soaking my jeans and sweater. Weather fit only for ducks and rabid outdoorsmen.

Down the hill I see evidence of spring's arrival. No longer is the overgrazed hill a murky brown of dead grass roots and mud clumps. The light green of new grass gives the hillside a much-needed facelift. The grass will be up to my waist by the first part of July — the natural fertilizer, accumulated throughout the winter, will give back to the earth what the horses took away.

I wonder if horses are blessed with common sense. On top of the hill I can see the three brown mares all standing within twenty feet of each other, contentedly grazing on young sprouts in the drizzle. Their winter coats, matted with mud and falling out in places to make way for their lighter spring fashions, look saturated with water until closer inspection reveals tiny rivulets running off the sides of their bellies. Their water-repellent fur keeps them immune to the soggy inconvenience of spring rain.

The gray barn holds vigil over the two acres of fenced pasture and the earthy mares. Ten years of inclement weather has made the wood, cement and corrugated roofing look fifty years older. Sagging under the sprinkle, the waterlogged structure sits at the bottom of the hill amid the muck and mire of a horse pasture. Deep green and iridescent blue interrupt the grayness as a determined mallard tries to attract the attention of his mate.

The rain is light but in a short time penetrates my jeans and a decided chill takes over my body. I crawl through the fence and head down the slippery hill. My slick-soled riding boots offer little traction.

Apparently I'm not the only one who has had problems. Telltale skids reveal the story of a scuffle earlier this morning between pasture mates. Four skid marks, three feet long and evenly spaced, mark where the loser, trying to escape the raging onslaught of her attacker, discovered the unstable properties of wet grass.

At the bottom of the hill I am greeted by wet brown muzzles looking for sweet treats. When the friendly giants realize I bear no gifts, they wander off, turning their mudcaked tails to me. Fair-weather friends, I think.

Wading through the muck, trying not to disrupt the romantic interlude of the ducks, I pry open the rusty latch and push open the chewed barn door.

Tempest, the youngest and prettiest of the three, tries to follow me into the dry interior in hopes of finding some remnants of hay on the concrete floor. Older sister Kismet bullies Tempest back outside. Since she is my horse, Kizzy thinks she gets preferential treatment, and she does. Her agile muzzle quickly goes to work on the alfalfa leaves and bits of grain that fell over the stall doors during this morning's feeding.

The barn is dark and damp. A sweet musty aroma, flooding my nostrils with an acrid tang, tickles my nose and send me into a flurry of sneezes. Through the dark I can hear the skittering of little feet and catch glimpses of gray tails and furry haunches running for cover. They have been caught nibbling on the leftover grain.

The caretaker of the barn and horses has left the "scooper" lying in the middle of the aisle, or perhaps it was propped against a stall wall and one of the delinquents threw it into the middle. I've seen the horses do things "expert horse-people" say are impossible. They have opened stall security latches, thrown pitchforks and pieces of wood around, turned on lights and caused general mayhem.

The alfalfa leaves quickly disappear inside Kizzy's mouth. Deanna, the third mare, joins Kizzy. Tempest is allowed back in. A chorus of crunching and grinding echos through the barn; wet muddy fur and sweet hay fill the air with a heady perfume.

Before too long, the horses shuffle back outside. The barn floor has been swept clean. Spring grass offers more tasty tidbits to fill their stomachs. Kizzy is no dummy, though. The residual hay and grain may be gone, but she knows that I hide the real stuff in the loft. She disappears out the door, only to reappear in her stall. She leans her large head over the stall wall and nickers, "May I have some more, please?"

The others hear her and soon three brown heads are peering at me over their stalls.

A little more hay from upstairs is all it takes to fill the barn with another chorus of Nature's own equestrian symphony. They begin separately, but soon blend together as one. The soothing cadence of each note rises and falls, separating and coming together again with the rhythm of the rain.

I pull a bale of alfalfa down from the loft and seat myself near the open barn door. I listen to the patter of rain on the roof and watch it mist outside. No, I can't ride today. But what does it matter? Riding isn't the only reason I come out here.

SAINT ISIDORE'S HARVEST

BY JAMES G. POWERS, S.J., Ph.D.

GRANT GOODLOE NEVER LOOKED MORE SERAPHIC. HE WAS found in his space-saver rocker as upright as a spring groundhog testing the sun. The cuff of the blood pressure gauge sagged loosely around his right arm, registering *zero*. Grant's perplexing smile, his wife concluded, could only be related to that little monitor, his constant companion, whose first optimistic readings invariably sent him into paroxysms of anger, challenging its accuracy and imputing its honesty. However, by the time that Grant savagely tore the sleeve from one arm and cinched it to the other, re-testing his condition, the systolic reading, acquiescing to its owner's dire prediction, had soared, like an Apollo rocket, to an alarming one hundred ninety, with the diastolic trying to rival it.

"Just as I thought!" he would bellow. "My pressure's out of control, and no damn machine can weasel out of the fact!" Designed to safeguard health, this impish device, accommodating its owner's anxiety, eventually killed him, coaxing his cerebral arteries to pop like bubble gum, stretched beyond its limit by a mischievous child.

Just at lunchtime, Estelle Goodloe discovered her husband's jauntily erect corpse. She breathed a prayer of thanksgiving, carefully returned her deviled egg sandwich to the refrigerator, then clutched the phone and dialed two individuals: Monsignor Morris Bledie, Saint Isidore's pastor, and Doctor Eldon Scurry. The latter was Grant's long-suffering cardiologist whom his former patient fulminated against on the average of once a month for his sanguine assurances that an imminent demise was only a creature of his sulphurous fancy.

The good cleric, who had refereed many a skirmish between these two gladiators, arrived first, to mediate their final separation. He perfunctorily administered the Church's last rites to the victim — "conditionally, of course, Estelle, because we can never be sure when the soul bids final farewell to the body."

"You can be in this case, Father," muttered the widow. "I can't imagine Grant's soul wanting to stick around one minute longer than necessary!" Then, noting her pastor's use of the word "conditional," she confided: "You gave me quite a start. For a moment, I thought you might be suggesting that there was a chance the poor devil could make a comeback."

"Oh no, Estelle," hastened the Monsignor. "I was merely implying that one's transition from this world may not be as instant as *Sanka Coffee* or *Prem Cream*, if you pardon the comparisons."

This assurance spared the priest from administering the same comforting sacrament to Estelle, whose pulse, always quite erratic, settled down to a contented rhythm.

As puzzling as an Internal Revenue form was how these two combatants became acquainted, engaged, and eventually married. Their association could only be described as a "connubial blitz"; relentless assaults were occasionally relieved by a smoldering truce. Oddly, each seemed to thrive in this war zone, as if the only intolerable alternative would be a marooned exile, far from the trenches of belligerence.

Grant refused to accompany his wife anywhere: "Travel's for them that have no home," he would grunt. His conversation, with the exception of an occasional growl, was sparse: "A mouth's to eat with, not gabble," he would snort. Likewise, his awareness level never extended to surprising his spouse with a gift, unless it was some gratuitous hectoring on household management: "Money's for saving, not squandering," he would snap.

Estelle too, over the years, had learned to confront her antagonist with the brittle severity of an attack dog trainer. Fortunately, she had worked consistently since her marriage, so was unaccountable for the clothes she purchased, the meager entertainment she enjoyed, and the modest treats she relished. In a word, apart from those staples whose expense they divided with all the bounty of a wolf pack, each walked a hermit's path.

Occasionally, Estelle, desperate, would dramatize profound disgust with her lot. One memorable Christmas she drew a skimpy holiday decoration to grace her beloved's spartan supper table. With lipstick, she sketched a desolate Christmas tree on a paper plate, and embellished it with a single ornament, hanging forlornly from a spindly limb. Finally, she fastened a plastic compass to the base, with the inscription: "A gift — for the hopelessly lost." This trinket she gingerly tossed on the kitchen table before departing to her brother's for some attempt at Christmas cheer. Upon her return, Grant, fidgeting with his blood pressure cuff, reminded her that it was her turn to take out the garbage.

Steaming into the kitchen, she discovered a "festive" scrawl on the sack: "Season's Greetings! Santa."

No wonder, then, that Estelle was not in need of Noah's ark to carry her safely over waves of remorse on the occasion of her husband's exit. Besides, she was soon to learn, astonishingly, that despite himself, Grant was to provide her with an unparalleled White Christmas, forever transforming her life.

Grant may have been bankrupt in love, but was surprisingly resourceful in insurance. Particularly attractive was a policy which matured upon the death of either spouse. Because Estelle for years had scuffled with a vexing heart condition, exacerbated, in Doctor Scurry's opinion, "by domestic tension," the policy held a unique proviso: its dividends would be more plump on the slim chance that her husband should retreat from this world first. Despite his challenging bouts with induced blood pressure, Grant felt confident that his wife would precede him into eternity; furthermore, since, in large part, he orchestrated that "domestic tension" which pestered their physician, he did not dismiss the prospect of facilitating her journey at any time he felt the odds slipping against him. In brief, he always presumed that the fruits of this premium insurance would be harvested by him and not Estelle, whose tenure in the orchard of life he viewed as ephemeral. However, the juiciest yield fell into Estelle's lap when her husband's stroke brought her a stroke of luck: the ripe dividend of two hundred thousand dollars.

"Yes, Estelle," puffed the venerable Monsignor Bledie, through grooved cheeks which looked freshly tilled. "Though your life with Grant was not the happiest, God has now chosen to reward you with the fruits of this earth. Husband these well, and, relying on good Saint Isidore, patron of farmers, be like the wise man of the Gospel who stored up produce in seven years of plenty for seven years of famine."

Estelle, more composed than at any time in her married life, sat reflectively in the shepherd's tidy but weathered rectory and absorbed his words. "I welcome your advice, Father. Believe me, I will not squander this abundance; I will not let it lie fallow in the ground, as the foolish man in the parable who buried his talents. This I promise, Monsignor: if the good Lord continues to favor me, I'll generously help Saint Isidore's reap plenty, so our dream of a new church can finally be realized."

"We can only pray," murmured the priest. "Now, may I ask a difficult favor? On the subject of prayer, let's not forget Grant — that the Lord will shower him with much-needed compassion."

"'Shower?' A deluge more than likely will be required!" exclaimed the widow. "However, I'll try, Father, but only because I know the Lord's store must be enormous, especially in the commodity of mercy. Still, I don't want him to exhaust His supply on one poor wretch."

Thus the colloquy, which followed Grant's interment, concluded, and Saint Isidore surely smiled: the seeds planted on this occasion were not scattered on barren rock, but in particularly fertile soil.

Weeks moped by and found a preoccupied woman thumbing through investment sources, like *Forbes* and *Fortune,* in addition to seeking fiscal advice from friends and references. Estelle ransacked her brain for lucrative schemes. Like Seattle rain, proposals were plentiful, but none really whetted her appetite, persuading her to commit her insurance bonanza to future prosperity.

Then, in the middle of one memorable night, the answer startled her with the insistence of a shrill smoke alarm. "Of course!" she bolted upright, warbling with delight. Grant would have worshipped it! A substitute "wife"! A blood pressure monitor with a reassuring voice. A loving recording to replace a dial's frosty reading. This is it! An affectionate gem . . . a doting partner to sooth and comfort all the Grants of this world! She rambled on excitedly to herself: "Why, such a marvel can be modeled after those popular new cash registers in Zelanski's Supermarket, which pleasantly chime: 'Cabbage, thirty-four cents a pound' and 'Bumble Bee Tuna, fifty-nine cents a can!' My voice can be just as silken, confiding if one's blood pressure settles at normal, marginal, or dangerous levels. Think of it! A caressing nurse and mother and lover in one guardian of health. In fact, I'll call it 'Grant's Guardian Angel.' Even *he* could cozy up to this mate!"

Rhapsodic, Estelle bounded from bed, convinced that Fate, or perhaps Saint Isidore, importuned her to open her door to Fortune and invite it in. So, after months of design, production models, marketing studies, and advertising, the miraculous gadget finally tumbled onto the shelves of prominent outlets. The first inventory sold out in less than a month, pressing the manufacturer to double his next stock. This too was rapidly depleted, with back orders choking the computer.

Soon, Estelle's creation was found snugly entwined around the arms of a large male population. These gaily colored monitors were rarely far from the anxious reach of husbands seeking affirmation in their health quest. Every zealot would gently slip the supple sleeve over his forearm, hugging the artery, and squeeze the pump until two hundred registered. At that level, a dulcet tone would intervene: "That's fine, Dear, don't squeeze too tight." The needle then would stutter downwards to sundry systolic-diastolic markings. If these ranged in the "safe zone," melodious words would coo: "Congratulations, Lamb! You're VERY normal." Marginal case readings were no less charmed by: "Good, Darling! But we CAN improve." In those worrisome cases of hypertension and its alarming surges, a mellifluous accent would urge: "Sorry, Honey. Your reading is high. Relax for ME!"

All in all, this solicitous "companion" exerted an almost mystical influence over troops of frayed junior executives, harried taxi drivers, frustrated retirees— all of whom sought to be eased, or coaxed, through each frenetic day. In short, their fervent interest earned Estelle interest with each healthy bank deposit.

Despite her acquired affluence, she did not forget her promise to Saint Isidore, and the saint, good husbandman that he is, must have looked benignly on his client, especially as he viewed his new edifice, largely brought to fruition through her pledge.

Strangely, in the seven years that had favored her business venture, Estelle had never been tempted personally to toy with her wondrous product, which so many clung to almost as a surrogate lover. Doubtless, her disdain of the device stemmed from Grant's exclusive fixation with blood pressure in earlier, dour days. Furthermore, since her husband's demise and her triumph bearing his name, Estelle felt that her health problems had largely dissipated.

"Unlike the Grants of this world, I don't need a 'sweet-talker' to tell me what I already know: that my heart is as sound as my bank account." However, her euphoria was premature. Bleak events wriggled free from the hands of protective gods and were grinning mischievously in her direction.

Another Christmas season, the seventh after Grant's dismissal, paid a visit like a sorcerer. A stunningly white one it was. Pillows of snow were tucked into every branch. Houses were dressed in pearl-like ruffles, their eaves sparkling in bonnets of frost. Milky strands of electric wires joined residence to residence, each plunged into a silence where every sound was outlaw.

The holidays invariably saddened Estelle, and so she sat alone, subdued before the indolent glow of her fireplace, nostalgically listening to seasonal music, which evoked somber, even bitter memories. Despite herself, her eyes brimmed with tears as she absorbed the lyrics to *White Christmas*.

Unconsciously, her glance moved over some boxes containing the one "present" of Grant's which had, in an ambiguous life, brought enrichment — her cherished invention, set aside as gifts for a few friends. She curiously reached for one, fondled it, and immediately, vividly thought of Grant. Mechanically, she untied the wrapping, stroked the mechanism, and, following his ritual, slipped the sleeve through her arm, secured it, squeezed the bulb, and permitted the arrow to climb to its proper level. Then, alarmingly, she noticed only a significant dip in the reading; in fact, the arrow careened upward, straining dangerously high! Suddenly, a voice, glacial and derisive, interjected: "Too high, Estelle! Dangerous, Estelle! Season's Greetings . . . Daaarling!"

Like an epileptic, the needle convulsed wildly, ruthlessly inching upward. Estelle could not shake off the strident, piping mockery, unmistakably Grant's. "Dangerous, Estelle! It's killing, Estelle! Santa says 'Season's Greetings'. . . Daaarling!"

Then, as if a dancing, electric coil were slashing at her arms and legs, she felt as though she were on fire; numbness disarmed every sinew and tendon. Her head throbbed, as if a dozen truck bumpers were pounding at the walls of her skull, only to reverse themselves and batter them again. Her eyes, like opaque doorknobs, grotesquely protruded and revolved slowly in her head, gazing blindly around the room. Finally, "Grant's Guardian Angel" sank from her arm, its glass dial impishly reflecting the purpled fact of its former owner. She was discovered sitting primly, if not quizzically, in the same chair which earlier witnessed her husband's departure.

Monsignor Bledie sadly celebrated the liturgical Burial Mass for Estelle Goodloe. In his brief homily, he praised her for the generous bequest which would vastly assist Saint Isidore's Building Fund.

" 'Estelle,' you know, means 'star' " he explained to the hushed congregation. "It is proper in this Christmas season, when we remember that wondrous star which shone over a small residence and glittered upon a Miracle, that today another 'Star' should shine over our modest house, witnessing something miraculous as well — the birth of our new church in honor of Saint Isidore, patron of plentiful harvests." At these words, his flock nodded joyous assent, blessed themselves, and murmured 'Amen.'

SAVITTS'
RIGHT WAR

BY DON D. MASTERS

THE VILLAGE LAY SWADDLED IN HEAT. LEAVES DROOPED IN the humid air and even the birds had ceased their twitter. The one hotel, a two-storied wooden building, grainy with age, faced the tree-lined square. Rorick sat at the bar on the veranda nursing his drink; he was the only customer. Behind the bar, Sancho, the old barman, jerked awake on his stool. He blinked then nodded to the wide stair leading up from the square. "*Americano,*" he said softly, breaking the silence.

Looking cool in pressed army green, the young first lieutenant strode to a table close to the bar, pulled out a chair and sat facing them. "You an American?" he asked Rorick straight out.

"I am if California hasn't seceded."

The young lieutenant laughed and pointed to the extra chair. "Buy you a drink?"

"Sure!" Rorick downed his *cuba libre* in a gulp then signaled to Sancho to make it a double.

The lieutenant put out his hand as Rorick sat. "Dan Savitts. I'm with the American Military Advisory Commission."

"Steve Rorick. Welcome to Tonichi."

"Thanks. Would you believe, we've been here three days and yours is the only welcome I've heard."

"There's a lot of guarded feeling in the country," Rorick explained. "Especially toward Americans." He looked at Savitts' smooth pink cheeks. There was no trace of a beard. Was the kid even twenty-one?

"It was the elected government who invited us here," the lieutenant was quick to point out. "Anyway, it's good to find a Yankee face."

Rorick smiled and said nothing. Elected by bribes and twisted arms, he had wanted to say.

An oligarchy of fifteen families ran the small banana republic of Condoro. With their rigged election they had crushed the Reformist party, driving Ramos and his fellow insurgents underground.

"*Señor?*" Sancho stood at Savitts' elbow. "What you drink, please?"

"Whiskey and water tall, a little ice," Savitts rattled it off.

"*Pardon, Señor?*"

Rorick rephrased the order in Spanish. "Sancho understands a little English," he told Savitts when the old barman had gone, "but you have to speak slowly and keep it simple."

"You live here?"

Rorick shrugged. "Yeah, I suppose you could say that." He saw Savitts weighing his answer and added plausibility. "Here on a prospect," he smiled. "Mining . . . lot of mineral in the country." The kid lieutenant had invited him over for a drink; broke and thirsty, he was grateful.

"*Señores.*" Sancho served the drinks and waited while Savitts hauled out a roll of Yankee green.

The lieutenant winked at Rorick. "Don't know about you," he said, "but I'm thirsty." He peeled off a twenty and held it up. "Yankee dolla' okay?"

"*Sí!*" Sancho beamed.

Savitts handed over the bill then laid a finger on Sancho's ample belly. "You keep. We drink. When money gone you tell me . . . Understando? What's the word?" he said to Rorick.

"*Comprende.*"

He looked up at Sancho. "*Comprende?*"

"*Sí! Sí!*" The old barman's face broke into a gullied ruin.

"Well, now . . ." The lieutenant raised his glass. "This is more like it. You can't beat the amenities."

"Your camp seems pleasant enough." Rorick nodded toward the square. At its far end on the outside under the trees, three neat rows of tents stood sun-dappled in the partial shade.

"Yes . . .it's pleasant," Savitts agreed. He looked at Rorick, his eyes heavy-lidded. "Cheers."

"*Salud.*"

They drank.

The lieutenant set his glass down with deliberate care. "I've been trying to remember California's official motto."

"Eureka."

"That's it . . . and the state flower . . . I've forgotten that, too."

"Golden poppy."

Savitts looked hard at Rorick. "Ever had any military experience, Steve?"

Rorick nodded.

"There's a ridge across the arroyo from our camp . . ."

"I know the place."

The young lieutenant leaned forward. "Can you imagine a battery of mortars dug in there?"

Rorick could. "Your camp is pleasant," he said, "but vulnerable."

"Exactly . . . it's no secret." Savitts sat back, frowning. "When Major Jarvis, our commander, bitched about it, the local comandante who assigned us the site told him, 'Is no worry. No *problema*. We control here.' Bullshit! That fat ass couldn't control a sick dog!"

"Been pretty quiet here lately," Rorick encouraged.

"That's part of the problem. It's been too damn quiet. We know Ramos is up to something. But we've no intelligence we can act on . . ." A dark flush had mounted Savitts' pink cheeks. "You know what the real enemy is here — besides the insurgents?" His voice rose in agitation.

Rorick was reluctant to ask. "What?"

"Apathy! Sloth! Incompetence! Nobody gives a shit!"

In the quiet drowse of siesta the words rang so patently true Rorick almost laughed. Instead, to humor Savitts, he nodded in sober agreement.

A sudden clump of boots made them turn.

From the hotel's dim interior a lone *campesino* stalked into the bar. Like all peasants he wore a faded serape draped over one shoulder. His battered sombrero, pulled low, was sweat-stained and caked with dust. A saddle-colored enigma, he stood at the far end of the bar, silent as the blue smoke curling from his cigarillo. Sancho hurried to serve him.

Savitts looked the newcomer over and said softly, "At least that one's not sleeping."

"Probably just woke up."

The lieutenant shook his head. "I don't understand. We come down here to help these people dump this Ramos prick and everybody knocks off to snooze. Ramos must be laughing in his tequila."

"More likely, he's snoozing too." Rorick waited till Sancho served the new customer then set his empty glass in the center of the table.

Savitts turned to Sancho, whistled and raised two fingers. "How do I say two more in Spanish?" he asked Rorick.

"*Dos más.*"

Savitts barked it out.

The old barman scurried from his stool. He was worried. He wished the *campesino* would go away. There was something taut in his stillness.

He didn't like gringos either, but at least they brought money. Not Rorick. *Señor* Rorick was *simpático* but he had no money. The baby lieutenant had no *simpático,* but he would leave on the table the price of many tortillas. Life was funny. As he mixed the drinks the *campesino* motioned for him to come. He palmed something across the bar. While his dark eyes commanded, his lips mimed the words: Do it!

Sancho brought the drinks and fled.

"You seem to know your way around here pretty good." Savitts twirled his glass while he studied Rorick. "Been here long?"

Rorick drinking, shrugged. He raised four fingers, thought a moment, then put up his thumb.

"Years?"

Rorick nodded.

Savitts whistled and looked at Rorick with new interest. "Joseph and Mary! Five years in this dump . . . ! Mining must be pretty good?"

"Home is where the heart is," Rorick joked, hoping to end the quiz. He looked out into the square then raised his hand in greeting.

Savitts turned to look.

Coming down the path that led to the hotel a man was pushing a wheelbarrow full of raw meat. Aside from the crawling carpet of flies and a mongrel dog sniffing for scraps, nothing else moved.

"What's he going to do with all that cruddy meat," Savitts wanted to know, "bury it?"

"That's old Chepe . . . his cow died this morning and he's selling the meat before the heat gets it."

"Selling it!" Savitts, starting to drink, put down his glass. "Selling it here—at the hotel?"

"Has to. Hotel's got the only freezer within fifty miles."

"Christ, it's already fly-blown!"

The lieutenant was as fussy as he was feisty, Rorick decided. "More protein," he said.

Savitts snorted his disgust. "*Carne* means beef, doesn't it?"

"As a rule, yes."

"You better believe I'll check the shittin' menu here from now on."

Rorick laughed. "Order poultry—*pollo*—you can't go wrong."

Savitts looked unconvinced. He took a long pull from his drink then choked and spit into the glass. Something floated there. He roared at Sancho, who came rushing over. "Stinkin' cockroach!" he shouted, stabbing a finger at the drink.

"Ah, *Señor*—pardon, pardon!" Sancho fished for the right words. "Please forgive—I make you good wan."

"Make it a beer," the lieutenant growled. "*Cerveza* . . . Or do they bottle cockroaches too?" he snapped at Rorick. "God! How do you stand it here?" His pink cheeks had turned to a full-bodied claret.

"The drinks," Rorick answered truthfully. To the barman, he said, "It's okay, Sancho. *Fue un accidente.*"

Savitts looked at Rorick, whose wintry smile he failed to read. He waited till Sancho, still apologizing, brought the beer and left, then said, "These people—! You know we can't afford to make the same mistake here that we made in Vietnam."

"What's that?" Rorick was slow to ask.

"To have had the power and not used it . . ." The young lieutenant paused to consider, then qualified it. "That was the real tragedy, you know, the real shame of Vietnam."

Rorick didn't like the turn of Savitts' conversation. His rudeness to Sancho and now his blind probing of an old wound triggered a name he had tried to forget. "At Khe Sanh, during the Tet Offensive," he heard himself say, "we used all the power we had."

The young lieutenant perked up. He looked at Rorick with sudden respect. "You-were-at-Khe-Sanh!" The words rang like a sacred litany. "Five thousand marines under siege for a week, outnumbered four to one."

"Three," Rorick corrected. He had to smile. No one else had ever heard of Khe Sanh. And to be praised . . . ! Aside from the politicians, who didn't count, it was the first praise he had heard for attending that phony war.

"It was a shitty war," he said. Then he thought, I should tell him all wars are shitty. But he doubted it would dampen Savitts' ardor. He had known a few gung-ho types. From day one as untested kids till they went home as grizzled vets (or were blown away), the killing put a sword in their skivvies. Given the chance, they would off any slope in sight, enemy or not, just to raise the body count. He didn't think Savitts was that kind, but it didn't matter. What mattered was that the kid was loose with his money and a drink was a drink.

"We studied your war," the young lieutenant brought him back. "It didn't have to be a shitty war."

"Studied?"

"At Officer's Candidate School. That's how I know about Khe Sanh. I came up through the ranks. My old man was a marine; master sergeant, thirty years. He fought in Korea — Heart Break Ridge. My grandfather was army. Purple Heart. Omaha Beach — number two — the big one. I missed Vietnam. But this one —" A soft intensity entered his voice. "This one has to be right . . . this one is *my* war!"

Rorick felt a small sadness. How does this kind of shit get planted, he wondered. "You're here then to fight . . . ? I thought you were advisory."

Savitts didn't hedge a word. "We are. But things will escalate. Castro is arming Ramos. We know that. When it blows, we'll be ready. We'll do it right this time. You can bet on that!"

"Do it right?"

"I mean, no more Vietnams. If you enter a war, you incur a moral imperative to win that war. We learned that at O.C.S. You owe it to your country."

Rorick drank and said nothing. The heat engulfed them; it was getting too hot even to talk.

Savitts didn't seem to notice. "Look — Vietnam, what happened there, it wasn't your fault. You've nothing to be ashamed of. It was the people— they wouldn't stand behind you." He leaned forward, his boyish face flushed with zeal. "Listen, we're going to make it up to you, right here. You have my word."

Rorick thought Savitts was reaching for his beer. He wasn't.

"Let's shake on it," the lieutenant said.

His grip was firm and overlong as if some secret pact had been made between them. To get his hand back, Rorick had to give a little tug.

The lieutenant's mood lightened at once. "Let's have another," he said. "How do I order rum in Spanish? This beer isn't cutting it."

"*Dos ron.*"

Savitts yelled it out then explained to Rorick, "I have the afternoon free and — " He turned up his palms. "I guess this is it. Tonichi's cultural center . . ." With a sudden grin he leaned to Rorick. "Unless, of course, you know where the action is."

"Well, there's Rosalita's after sundown," Rorick offered. "Here girls are active enough if you don't mind the jigsaw blades."

"Jigsaw blades?"

"*Señores* — Pardon." Sancho was nervous. He set the drinks down without further comment and hurried back to his stool. When Rorick glanced his way he looked at the floor.

"Jigsaw blades?" the lieutenant pressed.

"In your urine. Never been burnt before?"

Savitts grimaced and shook his head. As quickly as it had come, his buoyancy vanished. He took a long pull from his drink, his eyes fixed on Rorick. After a prolonged silence, he said, "Okay, don't answer if you don't want to, but I've got to ask. What really brings a guy like you to live in a dump like this? There's no minerals here."

A boat, Rorick was going to say. But the look on Savitts' face dissuaded banter.

"It had to do with Vietnam . . . Am I right?"

Rorick reached down. A hollow plastic knock came from under the table. "Nam had to do with this," he said. "Just call me 'One-gone'!"

Savitts' surprise was genuine. "What a shitty piece of luck!"

"I get benefits," Rorick felt the need to explain. He saw a touch of pity creep into Savitts' eyes and despised himself for wanting to feed it. Bugger all! Tell him he's right; in a way, Nam did bring you here. Nam kept you busy while your poor grieving wife broke your balls with your best friend. Tell him because of Nam you'll never know if the son she bore is yours or Whosits', whose name you can't say because it makes you gag. Then explain to him: listen, lieutenant, losing a flipper is nothing. You gimp. So what? But with a pair of busted balls you're crippled in the head. You drift about. You get lost and don't give a damn. In time you founder like a ship rusting, on and on, until one day— well, here we are! Sure, go ahead, try telling that to a baby-faced hun hot to play war and thinks you're a hero. For a moment he thought to get up and leave, then remembered he was broke. Busted balls, your ass! Tell him the truth. Tell him: any more, it all has to do with rum.

Instead, he took Savitts' hand. Again it was outstretched across the table. But now his eyes had gone funny and his twisted mouth was trying to speak, but no sound came forth. Could a man get that drunk on a little whiskey, half a bottle of beer and a tot of rum? The rum! Rorick shot a glance at Sancho, but the old barman looked away, his mahogany face a noncommittal mask. Christ! A Mickey Finn in Tonichi! Savitts was reaching for help.

With the distant whump! whamp! whump! of the mortars, the *campesino* at the bar put up his fist, one finger raised. *"Uno!"* he shouted.

As if by magic, a small black hole appeared in the center of Savitts' forehead. It happened at the same time the mortar shells exploded in the American camp. The rifle's crack, too, unheard, had been simultaneous. Nice choreography, Rorick, in a daze, was able to think. He watched Savitts' black hole turn into a surrealistic rose, then craning his neck, stared at his spattered brains. Like scrambled eggs half-cooked, they dripped from the table behind him, three feet away. The mechanics of the dumdum bullet were no mystery here. Savitts was leaning back in his tilted chair, his glazed eyes staring at the ceiling. What held him up, Rorick was slow to see, was himself still clutching his outstretched hand. He let it go and the young first lieutenant crashed over backward into his own gore.

Rorick's vision misted. He blinked and was not surprised to learn that he was crying. His tears, he knew, were not for Savitts. They were for himself; he had tried but couldn't care.

"Señor! Señor!" It was Sancho. *"Vamos!* Queek!" From the bar he was pointing to a door that led to the alley. Rorick finished his drink and stood up. In the doorway, Sancho whispered, "They made me do it! The cockroach, too, they made me do it!"

There were two *campesinos* now. They stood looking down at Savitts. Rorick heard the first *campesino* say, "Ees true, gringo, theese time we do eet right!" The other held a rifle with a scope slung by the barrel across his shoulder. Savitts had been right about two things: they were vulnerable, and Ramos would be laughing in his tequila.

As Rorick stumbled out the door he heard another salvo. It was like a sound track from his memory: the mortar's whump! whump! whump!, the brief silence of the shells speeding to arc, then the gut-wrenching whistle of their descent. He waited, remembering, his sphincter tight.

There it was, right on target, the old one-two-three punch. He felt the earth-shaking explosions and fought against his rising emotion. It was the same mix of feelings he had felt losing a leg in Vietnam: shadings of terror, frustration and anger, a deep sense of the irreversible. Another salvo made his ears ring, his stump quiver. He listened for returning fire and heard none. A massacre!

He stood in the alley, tired and uncertain of where to go. The day stretched before him, hot, sticky and empty. He was already sweating. Emotion had sobered him. That was bad.

Then he was moving, his bonus leg hitching ahead with its peculiar swing-jerk motion. He would go visit Father Amez. Yes, a cool glass of wine would be nice.

STILL KICKING

BY JOAN DeCLAIRE

I WAS PLAYING HOPSCOTCH WITH SUZIE TARNOFF WHEN the fight erupted among our big brothers. We heard them yelling and ran to the front yard to see the tangle of teenaged boys tumbling through the mud and dandelions. I knew my brother Tim was in the thick of it. I could see his olive green sweater at the bottom of the heap, and his glasses lay broken on the sidewalk.

Suzie ran up to the crowd of neighborhood kids forming a circle around the fight, and I followed her. By the time we got there, Rickie Tarnoff, Suzie's oldest, yet smallest, brother had peeled himself out of the pile. But big, fat Paulie Tarnoff was still sitting on top of Tim's back. Tim wasn't moving.

Suzie broke through the circle and started to kick my brother in the ribs. Seeing my chance, I followed her again, and started kicking Tim too. I pumped my leg as fast as I could. Toe into ribs. Toe into thighs. Toe in back and gut.

Tim looked up at me and moaned. It occurred to me that he looked different. Was it because he wasn't wearing his glasses, or was it the blood on his face? Maybe it was because I was above him and it was he who needed *my* mercy this time.

"How could you do such a thing to your own brother?" my mother asked me later as she tended to the cuts on Tim's forehead.

I knew from experience that an eye for an eye never sat well with her. "I forgot," I said.

"You forgot?! What did you forget?"

"I forgot he was my brother."

Christmas. Weddings. Funerals. Now, whenever my family gathers, this story of betrayal and denial is repeated. My brother howls. My sisters snicker. My mother shakes her head and smiles.

At last summer's reunion, Tim's six-year-old daughter Mollie turned an innocent face up to the gaggle of relatives and asked, "How could she *do* that? Did Aunt Maggie really forget my daddy was her brother?"

"Sure, I forgot," I said. "It was a confusing fight. If you had been there, you would understand."

And everybody laughed some more. But Mollie's instincts were right. Nobody could forget.

All seven kids in my family went through the Cloverdale Public Schools, but it's Tim, the oldest, whom the teachers remember. "Class Clown," some said with fondness.

"Wasn't he the student council president his junior year? Unprecedented."

"Married that Italian girl who was Clover Queen his senior year. What was her name?"

Lois Simonetti.

My first glimpse of Lois was at the campaign party Tim held in the basement his sophomore year. Tim told our mother he didn't want any "geek nine-year-olds" standing around gawking, so I hid under the stairs to watch.

Lois stayed long after all the other kids left. She told Tim she wanted to teach him to dance. He wouldn't want to make a fool of himself at the dance where they announced the election results, she explained.

She played the record "Blue Velvet" by Bobby Vinton over and over again, and they danced in circles that got tighter and tighter. Then they stopped and Lois kissed Tim like I'd never seen anyone kiss, except in the movies. Tim didn't try to resist her. In fact, he seemed to want to swallow her up. How could they do that and breathe at the same time, I wondered. My legs started shaking at the sight and a wave of nausea swept over me. I wanted to burst out of my hiding place and make Lois leave, but I didn't dare. Instead, I curled down and put my head between my knees, forcing myself to stay quiet.

"I think he stuck his tongue in her mouth," I told Suzie Tarnoff the next day. "I can't believe my own brother would do that. It makes me sick."

"It's called 'frenching'," Suzie told me. "Everybody does it."

Still, I felt relieved when my mother objected to Tim's plans to marry Lois. I was with my mother when she took her case to Father Berry's rectory one Sunday after mass.

"It isn't that we don't like the girl," my mother told the priest in precise syllables. "But he's only eighteen and we want him to finish his education."

"Tim's going to be president," I added, trying to support her argument. I knew this was true because he kept a scrapbook of every newspaper clipping he could find about President Kennedy.

"Does Tim love the girl?" Father Berry asked.

My mother made a disgusted noise like a cat sneezing. "Love? What does a teenager know about love?"

"I saw them frenching once," I offered. That's when my mother told me to go wait in the car. When she emerged, I could tell it hadn't gone well.

"Love . . . ," she muttered as she drove home. "What does a priest know about love?"

Six months later, the whole family was making preparations for Tim and Lois' wedding, to be officiated by Father Berry.

My mother took me to a beauty parlor to have my hair done the morning of the event. At the reception, I danced with my Uncle John, who said I looked a lot older than eleven. But Tim didn't say anything. I don't think he even noticed.

A month after the wedding, Tim and Lois moved into a trailer near the university. Tim studied hard and did well. Political ambitions weren't his only incentive: boys who dropped out of college went to Vietnam. But he also had to prove to my mother that marrying Lois wasn't a mistake.

Jack Kennedy had been dead four years by the time Tim was accepted into law school. I once heard him tell my mother that more than half of his first-year class were former student council presidents. After that, he quit talking about a political career.

As we grew older, I watched time collapse. People as old as my mother and as young as my littlest brother became close friends. But within my own family, the pecking order was perennially intact.

A few years ago, when I discovered my husband was having an affair, I called my big brother long distance. Tim was outraged at first, then full of concern and advice. He spoke with masculine authority, spouting a time-honored bill of rights I wanted badly to hear. It's inexcusable. You don't owe him a thing. You deserve better than this. You don't need him. You should kick the bastard out.

I followed his advice and within weeks, I got what I wanted. Steve came back to me, humbled, remorseful, and ready to commit.

About a year later, I took a business trip and had a layover in Chicago, where Tim and his family lived. I couldn't remember when I'd had any time alone with him. I called him the day before and asked him to meet me at the airport for a drink. He might be in court, he said, but he'd be there if he could.

As the plane descended, I took out a mirror to check my makeup. Looking into my own eyes, I remembered my mother's credo against vanity. What does it matter how I look, I asked, like a habit. It's better to be plain. For some reason, however, I knew that meeting Tim alone was different, and I could feel the rules shifting. I put on fresh lipstick and went out to find my brother.

The airport was crowded and I searched the gate for several minutes before I heard him call my name. I turned to see him standing there in a blue pin-striped, three-piece suit and a dilapidated, wide-brimmed, gray felt hat. I don't know what surprised me more — the hat or the salt-and-pepper hair that poked out from under the brim and hung in long bangs on his forehead. His smile was radiant.

"Maggie! I didn't recognize you at first," he said, laughing. "You're so thin. And your hair . . . you look different. You look beautiful!"

I was so startled by his compliments, all I could do was give him a clumsy hug. "And where did you get that hat?" I asked, laughing too.

"It's an old friend," he said. "It keeps me honest when I'm working on a tough case. Listen, I hate airport bars. I think we have time to go to a little place not far from here, if you don't mind."

When we got to his sedan, he knocked a stack of books off the front seat. Then he held one up to show me.

"Sonnets," he said. "I've really been into sonnets lately."

Over the years, I had watched him try guitar, photography, scuba diving, mountain climbing, sailing, woodworking, weight lifting, and coin collecting. Why not sonnets?

"Have you been taking a class?" I asked.

"No, I've just been writing some."

"Well, that's certainly a place to start," I said skeptically.

He took me to a tiny Italian restaurant on a narrow street. The room was decorated in tones of soft peach. There were fresh flowers on all the tables. At two-thirty in the afternoon, we were the only customers.

The waiter, who knew Tim, but little English, lit the candle on our table. Tim ordered cabernet, then pulled a folded sheet of paper out of his inside breast pocket and handed it to me.

Written in perfect iambic pentameter were fourteen scintillating lines about a woman, each proclaiming his devotion to her.

"I'm impressed," I said, keeping my eyes on the paper, afraid to ask him anything about it.

"I wrote it about an attorney I work with," he offered. "Her name is Maura. I'm in love with her."

"Oh." I looked up, shocked, but tried not to let it show.

"She doesn't know," he said with a wide smile, pleased by his deception. "I haven't told her. I haven't done anything. Lois doesn't know either. All Lois knows is that I'm different. Alive, for a change. Excited. I feel more alive than I have felt in years."

I believed him because I had never seen him so animated. As we drank the wine, he told me about Maura's life. She was a divorced mother of three and an excellent trial lawyer. He and Lois had been seeing her socially and the two families had taken a vacation together the month before. They went camping in northern Michigan. It was so exhilarating for him to see Maura away from the office, to see her outdoors with her children, relaxed and happy. The hours he spent with her were precious to him, even though they were surrounded by their families.

"Why are you telling me this?" I finally asked him.

He stopped short. "I don't know," he said, and he didn't. "Because you're here. Because I want to. Because I thought you'd understand."

"I do," I said. And I did.

He knew I wanted to hear more. As he continued talking, I felt transported. If I thought about my own husband's infidelity, or about Lois, or my suspicion that my brother was treading on the slippery ground of addictive fantasy, it was only for a moment. Mostly, I let his story, the romantic setting, the wine, the sonnet, and his ethereal smile carry me away. To a place where a woman could be loved — no, wor-shipped — perfectly from afar. To a place where a man could be made holy by his passion.

The three hours we had together flew by and Tim whisked me back to the airport. Rushing through the terminal, he asked if he could hold my hand. It was an odd request. We were not a family of touchers. But having never denied him a thing, I gave him my hand and I felt beautiful as we rode the mechanical sidewalk out to the gate.

I thought about him often in the next few months, but I felt embarrassed by the way we had been together, so I didn't call. He didn't call me and I assumed he was embarrassed too. Lois and Mollie had birthdays and I sent cards as usual.

Then late one night I got a call from Lois. I was surprised to hear her voice because we rarely talked on the phone. But I could tell in a minute that she was drunk and upset.

"So tell me . . . how did you survive it?" she asked.

"Survive what?" I asked back.

"Steve fooling around on you."

She knows, I thought, and felt it was I, as much as Tim, who had betrayed her.

"You just survive," I said, lamely.

"But you're still together. Steve came back."

"Where's Tim?" I asked.

"I don't know. Out somewhere. With someone. Things are falling apart. I don't know what to do," she said, her voice trailing off. Then abruptly she added, "What did you do?"

It took a moment for me to call the answer into focus. But soon it became clear. "I followed my brother's advice," I said, feeling defeated, feeling Lois' pain. And the image of Tim's radiant smile that afternoon at the airport was washed from my mind like a chalk drawing in the rain. I was back on the Tarnoff's sidewalk as I recited the prescription: kick the bastard out. You deserve better than this. It can't be excused. You don't need him. You don't owe him a thing.

Tim's birthday was the following week. Knowing he'd be hard to reach at home, I phoned him at his office. He seemed surprised, if not jarred, to get my call.

"I talked to Lois last week," I said slowly, gathering the courage to use words rarely shared in my family. "And I want you to know that I love you and I understand what you're going through."

"Oh, do you?" he said like acid. "Is that why you told her to get rid of me?"

"I did not!" I blurted, lying and wondering why. Why did he make me lie?

I wanted to hang up but he kept talking. He said he had been tormented by thoughts of Maura, obsessed with her. But when he went to her, she wanted nothing to do with him. In the meantime, his feelings for Lois were dying. Lois had been in a serious car accident a month before and had escaped unhurt. When he found out about the accident, he was neither frightened nor relieved. She might have been killed, but he felt nothing, he said. And even his feelings toward his daughter Mollie were changing. He saw her as a miniature Lois. He wanted to avoid her.

And lately, he'd been going out jogging along the highway near his house late at night. And he'd stop and just stand on the shoulder of the road, rocking back and forth on the balls of his feet, watching the cars go by, and coming face to face with the decision, over and over again as each one passed, whether to throw himself onto the road.

"Do you understand, Maggie?" he scolded. "Do you understand all this?"

"No," I said quietly, like a good girl who wants to give the right answers. And after I hung up, I added, "But I do love you, Tim."

That was about two years ago. Since that time, Tim and I have exchanged Christmas cards, pictures of our spouses, our children. We remember one another with store-bought birthday cards that say, "To a special brother," or "It's great to have a sister like you." When we're together — always insulated by the presence of other relatives — we talk about our jobs, our real estate, our vacations. And we retell the approved version of stories from our childhood.

But I've been thinking about it lately, and the next time Mollie asks about the fight with the Tarnoffs, wondering how Aunt Maggie could forget, I may tell her the truth. I'll say, "Mollie, you're an only child, so you may not understand this, but there have been lots of times I wished I could forget your daddy was my brother. Like when I was very little and he thought he had the right to use my butt for bongo drums. Or when I got bigger and he told me I had a nose like an anteater. And I believed him.

"And now that your daddy and I are grown up, and I want to talk with him about how crummy it feels to love somebody you've placed above yourself — somebody who always overpowers you — I can't say a word. Because in this family, we know that we don't talk to our brothers about love, and we certainly don't talk about how much it hurts.

"So, you see, I didn't really forget on that day at the Tarnoffs. It's just that the sight of him pinned down was too irresistible. When I saw my chance, I wanted to kick the bejesus out of him. So I did. And then I lied. But I didn't forget. I could never forget he's my brother."

WARREN'S THORN

BY BETTY J. VICKERS

ON THE MORNING OF THE CITY COUNCIL MEETING, WARREN awoke about as disgruntled as he'd ever been in all his sixty-seven years. That night the council was expected to grant a one-year conditional use permit to Neighborhood House, a residence for destitute women and children — which was fine with Warren except that Neighborhood House was right next door, just the other side of his neatly manicured laurel hedge.

"Why don't you try to accept the fact that Neighborhood House is probably going in and learn to live with it?" Anna said without looking up from the ironing board. "It would be different if you could do anything constructive about the situation but, truthfully, Warren, not even you can fight city hall — at least not and win."

Anna was a short, slightly plump woman who shared Warren's birthday, and had married him the day they both turned twenty-four. She had a trim coif of lustrous white hair that had never been dyed, and friendly brown eyes. People always seemed to like Anna immediately. She talked to strangers as easily as to an old acquaintance, and adapted readily to awkward circumstances — two talents Warren secretly admired but had never said so.

Warren frowned and shrugged into his old tan cardigan. "I'm not going to just forget it, Anna, and if I can't block the permit at the meeting tonight, then we'll sell this place. Put it on the market tomorrow, in fact. Ought to be able to move it fast with all my prize roses in the yard. Everybody likes roses, don't they?" He dropped his shoes on the floor, sat down at the table and began to pull on his socks.

Anna turned off the iron and replaced it on its heel. For a long moment she stared at her husband's bent, grey head. Then she went to the refrigerator and took out eggs for breakfast.

Actually, she felt sorry for Warren in a couple of ways. Although he had tried over the years to learn to be agreeable, he had more often than not failed in his efforts to make facile adjustments to things he didn't like. The one place he'd been successful was in the classroom with his high school students. He'd easily won their admiration and respect, and had even managed to get along quite well with other faculty and school officials — a fact that often amazed Anna since she knew, from her own years of teaching, the difficulty of working in a public school system.

She was also aware that Warren's general inability to adapt had been painful. So even though the limits of her patience had been notably stretched on more than one occasion she usually tried to be supportive.

And she understood his frustration about the proposed halfway house. Warren loved their peaceful neighborhood. He had worked hard to make their retirement years comfortable and carefree. But she didn't agree that having Neighborhood House next door would be as catastrophic as her husband was convinced it would be.

"No, Warren," she said now. "We won't need to put the house on the market; don't even think it. We've lived here over thirty-five years. Mark and Ellie were born and raised in this house, and now you would give it up *and* your prize rosebushes just because you've made up your mind not to like a new neighbor? No, I don't think so."

"It's not just *a new neighbor*," Warren fumed. "Try a whole passel of new neighbors — battered women and their shirttail kids all living under one roof."

"Oh, Warren, it won't be —"

"Did you ever stop to consider," he interrupted, "the amount of noise a crowd like that can generate? And as for my roses, well, their days are numbered anyhow what with those kids coming over here trampling them to mulch. We won't be able to leave the house without worrying about what's going on here. It will be one giant headache from start to finish."

Anna put the jar of fresh strawberry jam on the table and two slices of bread into the toaster. She'd heard these arguments numerous times, and was weary of trying to reason with him.

"Not me, Warren; you. You'll be worrying about the roses just like you do every day of your life no matter who's living next door. If it's not depleted soil it's aphids, and if not aphids then it's mildewed leaves on your show *Tropicana*. A couple of little homeless kids from Neighborhood House won't make any difference." She hadn't meant to sound derisive, but neither had she been able to mask her exasperation.

Warren hitched his chair closer to the table and poured milk into the steaming coffee mug. He shook out the morning newspaper and pretended to read the front page. Then he turned back to his wife. "Look, Anna, we're not talking about rosebushes here. We're talking about our right to live in a residential neighborhood, not one with a business operating right next door. And we're talking about peace of mind. Are you telling me you're really not going to mind living next door to that type of people?"

"What type of people?" asked Anna, pausing with the plate of eggs in hand. "You mean women whose husbands have been laid off, and who have no place to go with their children while their husbands look for work? Women and kids who would have to sleep in their cars — those who still have cars — without a place like Neighborhood House to go to?" She set the plate before him with a gentle thud. "Come on, Warren; think about what you're saying. What's to keep our Ellie from being in this exact same pickle someday? Have you ever thought of that?"

Her voice had risen slightly, and she always hated it when that happened. Years of living with Warren had proved that arguing seldom changed his mind. He was better off left to sort things out for himself and then, in time, to come to his own peace. Well, sometimes he did and sometimes he didn't. It looked like this was going to be one of the latter. She dreaded to think of him speaking at the council meeting that night. Maybe she wouldn't go with him after all, she thought, but immediately knew she would go. Maybe her presence would settle him. Heaven knew he'd need some sort of calming influence.

"For cryin' out loud, Anna, be rational," Warren said around a mouthful of toast and egg. "That's never going to happen to Ellie because her husband takes care of her and the kids. Always has and always will. He's a responsible man." He swallowed the bite and took a gulp of coffee. "I'm telling you, Anna, there's something wrong with men who won't see to it that their families have food and a roof over their heads."

Anna heaved a sigh and sat down across from her husband. "It's not always a case of won't work, Warren; it's usually a case of *can't* work. There's a big difference. And what makes you so sure it won't ever happen to Ellie? Bob could get laid off, just like anyone else, and he *could* even leave Ellie and the kids —" Warren snorted and started to speak, but Anna held up her hand to stop him. "Now, yes he could; our family is not immune to life, you know. Or what if Bob died and he was without —"

Warren snorted again. "Now you're just being silly. You know full well that Ellie and the kids could come live with us — *if* that ever happened, which it won't."

"And what if they didn't have that option?" she asked and looked her husband square in the eye. "We're getting older and may not be around if she needed us."

Warren hated any reference to age. "Oh, will you please get off that age kick?" he demanded. "Besides, you're being irrational again and refusing to look at facts. Let's just take the noise factor: you like to take a nap most days right after lunch, don't you? Well, you could say good-bye to that since there'll be about forty kids yelling and screaming right outside your bedroom window. Plus you'll have to get used to a steady stream of people tramping in and out, in and out, like the biggest Holiday Inn in the country — *and* what about the danger?"

Now it was Anna's turn to interrupt. "Danger?" she asked incredulously. "What kind of danger are you talking about?"

"I'm talking about all the violent men roaming this neighborhood looking for their wives and kids," he returned. "You can't tell me a good share of those women won't be battered wives, and that the police won't be over there day and night. I'm telling you, Anna, we're talking about trouble like you've never had to deal with before."

Anna stood up and began clearing the table. "Now Warren, you know the Director said Neighborhood House is not for battered wives," she reminded. "The Salvation Army has a place in town for abused families." She squeezed liquid soap into the sink and turned on the hot water. "Besides, they'll be limited over there to five or six mothers at a time. Now that's hardly the biggest hotel in the country, is it?"

Warren leaned back, crossed his arms over his paunch and scowled through wiry, overhanging eyebrows. "What about the value of this house and property?" he retorted, ignoring Anna's point and taking a new tack instead. Without waiting for an answer he rushed on. "I'll tell you what about it; it'll go to rock bottom in a New York minute, that's what. Why, we won't be able to sell it to save us."

"Then it won't do any good to put it on the market tomorrow, will it?" Anna said and smiled.

Warren was not amused and he was not in the least bit mollified. "Anna, this is not funny," he huffed. "This is not a joke that can be laughed off. If you don't care about our financial security anymore, then it's a good thing I do."

Anna laid the dish towel on the counter and went back to the table. She pulled her chair close beside Warren, sat down and patted his leg. "I'm sorry dear," she soothed. "Of course I care, but you seem to be making more of this than the situation calls for, now don't you think so?"

Stony silence. He refused to look at his wife.

"I know there's bound to be some problems," she continued, "but it does no good to dwell on them, and things have a way of working out, given a little time."

"There's just no use talking to you, Anna — you and your bleeding heart," he added, but without conviction.

She ignored the half-hearted taunt. "What's happened to your sense of humanity, Warren?" she coaxed. "I've known you to be responsive to people lots of times in the past — like with the last class of shop students you brought over to help build our gazebo just before you retired. Did they trample your roses or tear the house down, or anything like that? And whatever noise they made you were out there helping them make it, so how is this situation so different? Here you have needy people moving in right next door that you could —"

"*That's* my point, Anna." Now he turned toward his wife. "You just said it yourself: *right next door*. That's the corker. Now that I'm retired I ought to be able to kick back a little and enjoy life without having some *cause* stuck right under my nose. Let somebody else do the flag-waving for a change." His voice and eyes dropped. He picked at crumbs on the blue tablecloth. "I'm tired now, just plain tired, and I don't think it's asking too much to be let alone to live my own life."

Anna put her arm around his hunched shoulders. "Look, Hon, I know how you feel, but that's just it: we're *retired*, not all washed up." She rubbed his arm affectionately. "There's lots of good stuff left in us yet — you know that's true, don't you? Lots of top drawer stuff."

Warren didn't answer because even after forty-three years of marriage she could still melt him down when she talked all soft and furry like that. He reached over and took her hand. Maybe she was right, after all. He'd have to think about it.

After a moment, Anna got up and put on the sweater from the back of the chair. "I have to get over to my club now, Honey. We'll be sewing today making curtains for the bedrooms at Neighborhood Ho —"

"There now, you see what I mean?" Warren jumped to his feet and thrust his hands deep into his trouser pockets. "Now you're going to make curtains and after that you'll be over there hanging them. Pretty soon you'll be over there day and night, doing this and that and I'll be lucky to see you ten minutes out of any day. Now do you see what I mean?"

Anna didn't see what he meant, not at all. She picked up her purse and car keys. Pausing with her hand on the front doorknob, she turned to look at her husband. "It looks like we're never going to agree on this, Warren," she said quietly, "so you'll just have to do what you have to do and I will too. I'll sew the curtains and, yes, I'll no doubt help to hang them. I need to do whatever else I can to help out — both over at Neighborhood House and elsewhere — because I'm not willing to retire from life just because I've retired from the classroom."

She waited, but Warren's response was a silent glower. "I'll be home in time for lunch," she continued. "I've made some chicken salad and blueberry muffins, and I'd appreciate it if you'd put the kettle on to boil about half past eleven." She opened the door and started out.

"I suppose this means you're not going to the meeting with me tonight," he challenged, not wanting her to leave but unwilling to ask her to stay.

"No, Warren, it doesn't. I said I would go and I will." The door closed softly behind her.

"Humpf," he grunted as the car left the driveway and passed down the street out of earshot. Warren never took it well when Anna openly disagreed with him, and he suspected it was because she seldom ever did. He didn't see why she had to be so bull-headed this time. Couldn't she see this was no small potatoes issue? They both had a lot at stake here.

Suddenly his breakfast felt like a rock in the pit of his stomach, and he craved fresh air. He let the screen door bang shut behind him. Grabbing a can of rose dust from the porch, he marched down the steps and began squirting shrubs along the walkway.

"Rotten aphids," he muttered, "They never give up. Riddle a whole bush right before your eyes if you don't watch every minute."

Warren continued dusting shrubs along the walk, and then turned to the blooming gardens on either side. Pictures in his mind tormented him — visions of pesky kids and dogs from Neighborhood House invading his property to tear off buds and dig up roots. The knot in his belly seemed to grow with every gust of the insecticide.

When the can finally whooshed empty, he set the soaker hose going in the section with his prize *Pink Parfaits* and *Grand'mere Jennys*. Only when the work was finished and the empty can tossed into the trash bin by the back fence did he allow himself an angry glance at the big two-story house in the next yard.

Warren had to admit that the freshly painted white house with the green shutters did not actually look offensive. Yet he detested the sight of it. To him, it squatted over there like some bloated, somnolent machine just waiting for somebody to come along and start pushing its buttons to bring it to life. Then doors and windows would start banging open and shut. Delivery trucks would be rumbling in and out at all hours, stuffed garbage pails would attract barking dogs and get tipped over, and there'd be no end to the trouble and confusion.

Suddenly Warren felt exhausted. He stumbled into the gazebo near the old maple tree and eased down onto the bench. Closing his eyes, he leaned back and took deep breaths of the fresh morning air. Birds chattered in the swaying leaves overhead. The fragrance from dozens of opulent blooms filled his head and, for a while, he allowed himself to sink gratefully into the peace and familiar comfort of his own back yard.

The warning buzz of a passing bumblebee finally roused him. He straightened and flexed his stiff shoulders. As he leaned forward to stand up, his eyes fell on a nearby coral bloom nodding in the breeze. Its beauty grabbed him and held his gaze so that he felt powerless to look away. In a rush he was reminded of the time that bush had gone into the ground. It had been a retirement gift from his students, and they had planted it as a surprise the day the gazebo was finished. They hadn't bought just any old rose bush either. Somehow, the three girls in the class had found out what kind he wanted — probably from Anna, but she hadn't owned up to it — and had taken up a collection from the other students to help buy the bush.

Remembering those kids brought a keen sense of pride and pleasure. Premium bunch of kids, they were, and not a dud amongst them. Well, except for that little skinny guy. What was his name? Had great big feet he kept tripping over all the time. *Gunboats*, that's what the others called him, but he didn't seem to mind. All of his projects in shop class were disasters — drawers wouldn't close and doors hung open. But he'd worked his little tail off helping on the gazebo. He'd built the bench where Warren was seated and, although it had turned out wobbly, not quite true, the kid had been particularly proud of his work. Warren smiled as he gently rocked the bench to and fro.

And the three girls? Nobody could say they hadn't done their share of the work. Real troopers, they were. Held nails in their mouths just like some girls hold sewing pins, and hammered and glued just like anyone else. They'd done a bang-up job on the lattice work, too. And didn't they love the roses? Practically speechless when Anna cut them a bouquet of *Moniques* to take home. Couple of the boys wanted some too— to give to their mothers, they said.

Warren now realized how long it had been since he'd done anything much other than tend his roses. He also recognized that, for the first time since his retirement, he felt lonely.

Well, who was to keep him from inviting the kids over again and building another gazebo? Anna? Yeah, she'd say there wasn't enough room in the yard for another one, and she'd be right. Besides, those kids would have scattered to the four winds by this time.

What about a new tool shed? He could build one to look like a miniature chalet. But why? He already had one on either side of the house.

Maybe a lean-to over the trash bins. Warren frowned. He could put that together in one morning and, anyway, there was nothing creative about a lean-to.

Then what *could* he build?

Against his will, Warren's eyes traveled over the laurel hedge to the back yard next door. Sure, there was plenty of room to put up something over there, but what would they want with a gazebo? They wouldn't know how to appreciate it anyhow.

He discarded that idea along with the tool shed and the lean-to, and tried to think of other possible projects. In spite of himself, he experienced the almost forgotten surge of excitement that always preceded the resolution to start a new building job.

Even so, when the idea of the playhouse first crept into his head, Warren balked. He dredged up every argument in the book to try to talk himself out of it: it would be too expensive; it would encourage the kids to run riot on his property; they wouldn't know how to take care of the playhouse; Anna really would be over there all the time if he showed any interest in Neighborhood House.

But his rational mind countered every objection with answers like: nothing's cheap these days, but you know you could swing it; having their own playhouse would keep the kids *out* of your yard; kids don't have to *take care of* a playhouse; and Anna's going to help out over there anyhow, so what's the difference?

Still, Warren couldn't quite commit to the idea. He had to kick it around a little longer. What if the job turned out to be more than he wanted to do alone? He doubted that the kids would be of much help. But why couldn't they hand him things? — like hammers, nails, small tools. And wouldn't they still be after his roses when they saw the buds beginning to open? Not if he helped them plant some flowers of their own around the finished playhouse. Nothing fancy like the *Milestones* or the *Sunbrights,* of course, but maybe some dahlias and poppies.

The notion began to solidify. He was also beginning to get a different kind of vision in his head — including one of Anna. Wouldn't she be floored to find out she wasn't the only one who could do something over at Neighborhood House? Yes sir, he'd tell her about it today, right after lunch.

Well, maybe not *right* after lunch. Better leave himself some room to change his mind. After all, things like that had a way of getting out of hand, and he had no intention of painting himself into a corner. Probably wouldn't work out anyhow.

Still, it wouldn't hurt to rough out a plan now. Not necessarily to scale, but just to get some idea of how it could go together and how much cash it might take.

Back in the kitchen, Warren rummaged in the desk for a pencil and some graph paper. Then he sat at the table for a long time making drawings and adding columns of figures. When he heard Anna's car turn into the driveway at eleven-forty, he hastily stuffed the papers into the drawer by the sink. The burner was just beginning to redden under the kettle when Anna walked in the kitchen and greeted her husband.

"That rose catalog you've been waiting for finally came," she said, handing the stack of mail to Warren. She replaced her sweater on the back of the chair and reached into the refrigerator for the chicken salad.

A stranger wouldn't know it, but Warren knew his wife was still disturbed about the morning's discussion. To tell the truth, he didn't feel so good about it either.

In an instant, Warren made up his mind. Let the devil take the consequences if he tipped his hand before he was ready.

"Say, Anna, will you go with me to the lumber yard tonight after dinner?" he asked, before a case of cold feet could set in. "I want to pick up some supplies to start a project I've been thinking about —"

Anna looked at him quizzically.

"— for next door — over at the new place," he finished lamely. He hadn't been able to make himself say the words *over at Neighborhood House.*

Anna's eyes brightened momentarily, but she couldn't trust what she'd just heard. "I'm not sure I know what you mean," she ventured. "I thought you wanted me to go with you to the city council meeting tonight. Have you changed your mind?"

Warren walked over to his wife, took the silverware from her hand and laid it on the counter. "We might have something better to do," he said. Even though a hint of cold feet still threatened, he felt great. "Sit down here and let me show you what I've been doing this morning."

Then Warren took the rumpled drawings from the drawer, smoothed them out on the table before his grinning wife, and sat down beside her. Taking up a soft pencil, he began to sketch shrubs around the draft of the playhouse. "What kind of flowers do you think would work best here?" he asked.

GOTCHA!

BY LISA COURTNEY

LAW ONE: Always remember that the way a man treats his mother is a fair indication of how he is going to treat his wife.

LAW TWO: Never never never let your mother-in-law live within a day's drive of your house if you have any intention of living your own life.

LAW SEVENTEEN: Always keep the name of a professional assassin on your Christmas card list.

(excerpted from *SUSAN'S MARRIAGE SURVIVAL HANDBOOK*)

THERE WERE SEVERAL REASONS WHY I WANTED TO KILL MY mother-in-law. Actually, the reasons ran into the dozens, but it all boils down to the fact that Muriel Allensby needed to be shot. And then hung. Drawn and quartered followed by a tasteful hanging. And then maybe starved before being fed to wild dogs.

I would have done it, for free.

Rick, my husband, didn't see what the problem was. He *likes* his mother, most of the time. He will do just about anything to make her happy, including taking her out on dinner dates, meeting her at the movies and going to ball games. Muriel much prefers his company to *our* company.

"After all, Susan," she says, "Three is a crowd, and Richard was mine *first.*"

I wish she would choke on that delicate little laugh of hers.

Fortunately, he is not a perfect son; if he was, we never would have lasted. Muriel has been trying to subtly persuade him to leave me for most of the ten years that we've been married.

"Dear sweet God, Richard, how can you continue to live the way you do? There are no children in your house! Your wife doesn't take good enough care of you — just look at the shirt you're wearing! It looks like it's never seen an iron! There's dust on the television and I've never seen a vacuum cleaner here! Shall I hire a part-time cleaning lady? And you know Susan doesn't like me; all she does is hide in the garage and play with paint! And I never see enough of you, darling!" With little or no provocation, Muriel has been known to chant her litany. We can say it right along with her, word for word. I'm thinking of having it put to music.

Every time she starts, Rick puts his arm around her, kisses her on the cheek and says, "Mom, Susan and I are happy. We like our life just the way it is, and you see about as much of us as you want to. We met you downtown for dinner last week, and I was at your house moving furniture on Thursday night. Can I get you a glass of water or something?"

Rick is a great husband. He is also a good son. Muriel may have been a good mother; I can't tell.

They always had a stable relationship, made stronger by the sudden death of Rick's dad, some fifteen years ago. Muriel kept herself busy by devoting most of her considerable energy trying to run Rick's life. As far as she's concerned, things were moving along quite nicely until I came along.

Rick and I met, fell in love and married while Muriel was on an extended tour of Europe with a group of women from her church. She doesn't talk about it much around us, but we know very well that Muriel believes in her heart that Something Very Sneaky was going on; had she not been traveling, she could have stopped the wedding and made short work of the woman who took her Richard away.

Muriel is classically beautiful. She is a natural blonde, with big, expressive brown eyes and a selective smile. She is tall, imposing, slender and can be quietly elegant for the right audience. Her only physical fault is that she still wears eyeliner like Liz Taylor in *Cleopatra*.

You can look at Rick and know that Muriel is his mother. He shares her blond good looks, her smile, her height and her slimness. The major difference between them, apart from the obvious gender, is that Rick's eyes are a sparkling blue, and his sense of humor can be easily read in them.

I don't fit into the family portrait. I'm dark, and about six inches shorter than Rick. (I'm four inches shorter than Muriel but I have several pairs of very very tall shoes.) Rick says that my eyes are so black that he can see the midnight sky in them. He's got the soul of a poet. I love my husband.

I've never been crazy about my mother-in-law.

From the very beginning, Muriel has gone through phases where she will not call for weeks at a time; she uses me as an excuse to make Rick feel badly, which, as a dutiful and loving son, he manages to do with laudable consistency. "Susan was a bit abrupt with me the last time I called, so I thought I'd better stay away" and "I heard Susan making cracks in the background the last time so I didn't call because I didn't want to interrupt your lives. I know when I'm not wanted" are on her hit parade of guilt trips that still work on Rick.

On the other hand, Muriel has been known to call two and three times in an evening. I find this irritating but amusing, since she only lives thirty-five minutes from our front door.

But she doesn't call and ask Rick a quick question or try to get him to do something for her, she talks for an hour, like I said, sometimes twice a night, sometimes more.

When she doesn't call for weeks, Rick feels guilty and neglectful. When she *does* call, every day, every night, Rick and I argue.

Muriel has been a problem.

It is hard to have a conversation with your husband (or watch a movie or play chess) when your mother-in-law is on the phone constantly. It is even tougher to make love while the phone rings, while you're waiting for the phone to ring, or while he's talking to her *again*. I know. I've tried.

A telephone answering machine is *not* the answer. After more arguing than I want to admit, we leave the thing off when we're at home. Rick feels guilty because Muriel *knows* we're there ignoring her. She cries into the phone. It's pathetic.

One day last month, on a Monday night, Rick came home from work in a deliciously amorous mood. He came bearing gifts — roses and pizza.

I set the table, he opened some wine, and we sat in the dining room with the pizza, the roses and some small talk. The evening promised to be fun.

Rick reached for my hand across the table and squeezed it.

The phone rang.

I closed my eyes. "It's Muriel."

"It can't be," he said at the second ring. "She called me twice at the office today. I finally had to get a little tough with her so I could get back to work."

It rang again. He looked at me. "It's *not* her."

I was closest to the phone. I picked it up as I know Sarah Bernhardt would have. "Hello, Muriel, what do you want?"

Rick looked at me as if I were kidding.

"Of *course* I knew it was you . . . no, Muriel, this really isn't a good time. He can call you in the morning . . . No? Can he call you later this evening? We're right in the middle of dinner . . . "

Rick was mumbling at me. "Tell her I'm not here."

I handed the telephone to him. She had heard him and was working up to bursting into tears.

He frowned at me as he took the phone. "Hi, Mom!," he said, putting on that artificial cheeriness I detest, "What's up?"

Whatever was up had to have been a big deal. Rick didn't say anything but "uh-huh" and "hmmmmm" and "yeah, right . . ." for the next twenty-eight minutes. To be fair, he *did* try to interrupt her and get off the phone, but she wasn't having any of that. He was in for the duration. I took the bottle of wine, my glass and two pieces of pizza to the living room and turned on the TV.

When Rick finally joined me, he was full of gentle apology. "Sorry about that, Honey. Mom's life was falling apart because she thought I was mad at her for calling me at the office today."

I looked at him soulfully. "Big deal."

"Don't be that way, Suze. I'm her only child."

I sighed. "It's probably for the best. If she'd had five children instead of just you, she'd now be making *ten* people nuts instead of just the two of us."

He put his arm around me. "Don't warm to the subject of my mother. We have *plans* for this evening."

I studied him. He was still interested. I do not play hard to get. I let him kiss me.

"Rick?"

"Hmmm?"

"Let's take the phone off the hook or unplug it . . . "

"Why? She's already called and talked herself out. She won't call back tonight."

At moments like this, a vigilant wife can detect the presence of dead brain cells in a husband.

"Trust me, Rick — do that or put the answering machine on for a little while, so we can forget about everything but ourselves."

"If we do that, and she *does* try to call, she'll get upset."

"Too bad. If we *don't* take the phone off the hook, *I'll* get upset. This is my house. I win."

Tugs-of-war, like mothers-in-law, are not conducive to romance in my marriage.

"All right, okay," I told him, "If she calls, it is your job to get rid of her within fifteen seconds of 'hello'. I think she's on a roll — she's not done with you tonight."

"Susan, if anyone calls tonight, it'll probably be one of your friends wanting a little girl-talk."

I glared at him.

To be on the safe side, we held hands and watched TV for an hour.

The phone didn't ring.

We took a shower.

The phone didn't ring.

While Rick turned the house lights off, I put some soft music on in the bedroom, lit a couple of candles on the dresser and kicked the cats out.

We climbed into bed; Rick pulled me close and kissed me.

The phone rang.

"She has radar!" I screamed.

He chuckled. "It might not be . . ."

I picked up the phone from the bedside table and resolved that it would not be there tomorrow. "What do you need, Muriel? . . . Rick? No, Rick's not here, Muriel. He went someplace where there are only *orphans* and no telephones . . ."

Rick took the phone from me. "What is it, Mom? I thought we pretty much covered that earlier — " I mouthed at him *fifteen seconds* and pointed to the clock " — No this is *not* a good time, Mom . . . you can't just call every time — calm down, Mom . . ."

In that moment, somewhere between Muriel's ready tears and Rick's voice soothing her and telling her he was sorry he'd been rude, I decided that Something Had To Be Done. I had had it, and was not going to play the game any longer.

Something, I promised myself, was going to happen. But I knew I had to keep Rick out of it. The fundamental bond that Rick and Muriel share, positive and strong at times, delightfully tentative at others, was one that I knew better than to touch.

I'm not the kind of person anyone could call innocuous. That's the way I am. "When she's pushed too far," my friends say, "Don't be surprised by *anything* Susan says or does."

So, in a way, I am forced to misbehave. I have a reputation to maintain, dammit.

I spent most of that night thinking about it (after he spent close to another hour on the phone with his mother, I pretended to be asleep so he rolled over and was snoring in a matter of minutes). I knew I couldn't spill any blood, and that I couldn't do any serious damage; but I was determined to get Muriel's attention.

Before breakfast, I knew what I was going to do. I could hardly wait. Why hadn't I thought of it before?

After Rick left for the office, I showered, got dressed in my favorite blue sweater and jeans, vacuumed the entire house, and made myself a congratulatory cup of tea.

Then I called the telephone company, told them my name was Mrs. Allensby (well, it *is*, after all), gave them Muriel's phone number, and told them I was moving and wanted my telephone disconnected *today*.

The customer service representative I spoke with assured me that the phone would be out of service by midnight, and they'd generate my final bill.

Muriel would have no telephone. At least, she'd be out of my hair for a day or so. And maybe she'd get the hint. Even if my small gesture did no good at all, it had succeeded in making me feel marvelous: powerful, in control, and just a tiny bit like a rotten little kid. She'd have a fit, I knew; but that was all right. Rick, once she told him about it, would have a hard time keeping a straight face.

"Gotcha, Muriel," I said to no one in particular.

I spent the day in my studio (formerly our garage) painting with a burst of energy I hadn't felt in months. *The Wild Mare* was by far the best thing I'd done in years. She was fantasy-born; she'd cast a spell on me the first time I picked up the paintbrush. I quit at about four o'clock, not exactly thrilled with my progress but happy anyway; I'd been more focused on Muriel's reaction to her phonelessness than I'd been on the work. I wished I could see her face when she realized that she'd been cut off.

Rick got home around six. We had dinner, dessert, and went to bed early. I was fairly certain there'd be no interruptions from Muriel. If Rick had any comment to make on the barely concealed glee on my face, on the fact that I made no remarks about his mother's nightly call(s), or on my fairly smooth seduction, he wisely kept it to himself.

Later, as I drifted contentedly into sleep, I thought briefly of Muriel. Poor poor phoneless Muriel; I'd known her for ten years, and today was the nicest day she'd ever given me. I fell asleep with a smile dreamily stroked into my face. Rick saw it and thought he'd put it there.

I was in the studio two mornings later, lost in the colors of *The Wild Mare* when the phone rang. It would be Muriel, I thought. Well, I'd had my fun. I put the brush and palette down, wiped my hands off and lifted the receiver on the sixth insistent ring.

"Hello . . . "

I didn't know the voice on the other end of the line. "Hello? Is this the Allensby residence?" It was a woman's voice, cool, crisp, and professional.

"Yes," I said, "I'm Susan Allensby."

"Ms. Allensby, my name is Helen Mead, with University Hospital. Is Mrs. Muriel Allensby your mother?"

"Muriel is my mother-in-law. Is something wrong?"

Helen Mead had an efficient voice. "Apparently your mother-in-law had a heart attack late last night. She tried to call 911 for help, and her telephone didn't work."

My God. "Is she all right?" I asked, stunned.

"Yes, poor thing. She crawled out of her house, and made it to the home of her next-door neighbor before she collapsed. The neighbor called 911 and she's fine, resting comfortably. If all goes well, she'll be released first thing in the morning."

My head was pounding. I couldn't breathe. "I'll be right there — University Hospital, you said?"

Helen Mead was firm. "As I said, she's resting. She asked me to call you for her. We've got her on a mild sedative: we want her to stay calm. She wanted me to assure you that she'll call you this evening — she doesn't want you to worry. She'll come out of this all right."

My mind was spinning with all kinds of possibilities, not one of them pleasant. Wait until Rick found out that his mother could have died because she couldn't contact 911 because I had had her phone disconnected. I might have killed her. My heart sank somewhere between my belly and my Nikes.

"Ms. Allensby?" I'd forgotten about Helen Mead. "Are you all right? I didn't call you to upset you, just to let you know about Mrs. Allensby; someone in the family had to be told, you understand, and this is the phone number she gave me . . . ."

"No, no, it's all right," I stammered. "Please tell Muriel that we love her and that we'll talk with her tonight, then."

"Will do," said Helen Mead, and hung up.

I put the receiver back in its cradle and shook. Dear God, what had I done?

I staggered into the house and wandered into the kitchen. There was an unopened bottle of chenin blanc in the refrigerator. It was only eleven in the morning, but I didn't care.

I could hear the commercial. "Any time is the right time for chenin blanc . . . when you're having chicken, fish or when you're caught trying to murder your mother-in-law."

By twelve-thirty I had very little wine left but I'd calmed down considerably.

I'd played the scenario every way I could think of. Any way you cut it, I was entirely in the wrong. Rick would not think this was terribly funny. And someday, when the incident was nothing more than an amusing anecdote, Muriel would still have won. Her brush with death, with my prank as the icing on her cake, would guarantee that she could have Rick's attention for the rest of her life. No, this was not going to be fun.

At five minutes to one, there was no wine left in the bottle, and my perception of the situation at hand had twisted and stretched in directions I hadn't considered before.

Why hadn't the hospital called before now? Wouldn't they have called last night when she'd been admitted? Muriel and I were not even remotely close — why had she asked Helen Mead to call me at home when she should have had her call Rick at work? Something was not right. Who was Helen Mead, anyway? A nurse? An administrative assistant? "Helen Mead from University Hospital" didn't necessarily tell me anything, did it?

I needed to sober up — fast. My thoughts were coming too quickly, and I wasn't holding on to them long enough to work them all the way through.

I clumsily made myself a big sandwich (I hadn't eaten yet) and drank a big glass of milk, followed by a large cup of soup. After that, I stumbled into a jacket and went for a walk around the block to try and clear my head.

When I made it back to the house, I was ready to move into action. I hoped to God I was right.

I called University Hospital. "Muriel Allensby, please. She's a patient. She was admitted last night."

The switchboard operator asked me for a telephone extension number. I didn't have one.

She sighed; no one ever seems to make it easy on operators. But she checked for me anyway.

"There's no Muriel Allensby here, ma'am."

My hopes were on the rise. "Could you check Intensive Care and also Coronary Care? She had a heart attack last night."

The operator checked. No Muriel.

One more try. "Then could I speak to Helen Mead, please? She's not a patient; I think she's either a nurse or an administrative assistant . . . "

A couple minutes of checking with the Director of Nursing and also with the administrator's office proved that there was no Helen Mead at University Hospital. I thanked the operator for her kind help and hung up the phone.

Muriel had not had a heart attack. Muriel was fine.

Muriel had enlisted a friend to help. And I had been had.

The score was now one all.

When Rick came home at six, I was in bed already.

"Susan, you look awful . . . can I get you something, honey?"

I tried to smile at him, but my face hurt. "No, nothing, Rick. I'll be all right. I must have a touch of something." (A touch of chenin blanc, I groaned to myself.)

Rick sat down gently beside me. "You poor baby. You're so pale! Do you have a fever?"

"No, I just feel yucky. I'll be okay, really. I just need some quiet."

"I can take care of that. I think I'll unplug the phones so the ringing won't bother you, so you can get some rest, okay? And I'll make you something light to eat, and while we're eating, I'll tell you about my business trip."

Business trip? "Where are you going?"

"I have to fly back East for about a week. There's a problem with . . . "

But I wasn't listening. My mind was working again, sidestepping the headache. I interrupted him. "*When* are you going?"

He looked at me lovingly. "I'm supposed to fly out first thing in the morning, Suze. But since you're not feeling well, maybe I should call Aaron and see if they can get someone else to go — "

I am married to a saint. He is married to Hell On Wheels.

"Don't be ridiculous, Rick . . . I'm fine, I just have a killer headache. I've been working like mad on *The Wild Mare* and I probably overdid it with the fumes . . . of *course* you're going on your trip . . . I won't hear of you not going! But you're sweet to want to stay and take care of me . . ."

"I love you, Suze. You're the best. I guess I'll go, then, but I'm taking care of you now." He kissed me gently on the top of my aching head, and then he actually unplugged the telephone.

I didn't let him see my shock. I knew Muriel was going to call tonight, to bust the game I'd played and then to let him know that she'd gotten even. She might even beg him to never let me do such an evil, dangerous thing again. I could hear it: *If the situation had been REAL, Richard, I could have died.* She was going to call — and *not* get through! Rick himself had insisted that we would not be disturbed tonight on account of my chenin blanc-induced killer headache.

Maybe I'd been too hasty, I mused. Maybe I *would* drink chenin blanc again. My mind was suddenly less fuzzy, more fearless than it had been in hours. I could hear Rick unplugging the phone in the living room and the one in the kitchen. He wouldn't think about the one in the studio.

And even if it rang, he wouldn't hear it. He'd be with me, eating dinner, talking about his business trip, packing.

Just that easily, it hit me. RICK WAS LEAVING IN THE MORNING, leaving for a week.

Uh-oh. I could feel it surfacing; it felt fabulous.

Look out, Muriel.

Rick took off the next morning, hesitant to leave me even though I looked and said I felt much better. He promised to call me at bedtime every night and promised to take care of himself for me. He asked me to let his mother know (when she called) that he was gone on business. I kissed him and told him I would.

He wasn't out of the house fifteen minutes before I began plotting. I called his office and spoke to Brenda, the receptionist.

"Brenda, this is Susan Allensby. How are you?"

Brenda's a pleasant woman in her early twenties. "Fine, Mrs. Allensby. How are you?"

"Fine, Brenda, just dandy. Listen, there's something I'd like you to do for me. And when we're through, I'd like to talk to Jackie . . . " Jackie is Rick's secretary.

As they say, anything worth doing is worth doing right.

This was worth doing.

After I spoke with both women, I took a long shower, and worked out the bugs in my plan. Then I practiced a little, and got most of the giggles out of my system.

I put An Affair to Remember in the VCR, got a box of tissues and a bag of chips, and settled down to watch the movie.

The movie was over at two o'clock, and, as always when I watch it, I was in tears, weeping over Cary Grant and Deborah Kerr, almost unable to speak.

It was time to call Muriel.

She'd had her phone reconnected, as I knew she would. She answered on the third ring.

"Muriel?" I croaked, tears streaming down my face. "Muriel, is that you?"

"Susan? How did you know I was here? I assumed that you thought I was — "

"Muriel, Muriel, I need you. Something just awful's happened, and it's all my fault, and I don't know what to do . . . "

I had to be careful not do overdo it. I cleared my throat and made it sound as though I was struggling for control.

She hadn't gone for it yet, but she was listening. "What's going on?"

I took a deep breath. "I know you know I had your phone disconnected as a practical joke, Muriel, and I'm sorry. And about your heart attack . . . "

Muriel sounded proud of herself, but she isn't a stupid woman. "You know very well that there was no heart attack. I was just getting back at you for having my phone disconnected. How long did it take you to figure out that I — what's wrong, Susan?"

"I figured out that you were okay after I tried to contact you at University Hospital last night and they never heard of you."

"Well, let that be a lesson to you — "

Desperation and agony edged into my voice. I was beginning to screech. "Muriel!!! When I first got the call from Helen Mead — "

"One of my bridge partners," interrupted Muriel.

" — I called and told Rick about your heart attack and what I'd done to you — " she was listening now " — and he had some sort of seizure and Muriel — " my voice broke " — he died, Muriel. He's DEAD!!!"

"This is *not* funny, Susan. You ought to be ashamed of yourself. You're a grown woman."

"I'm not kidding, Muriel, you've got to believe me . . . "

Muriel was indignant, which told me that she was beginning to buy it. And to think my college theatre professor thought I didn't have what it takes to be an actress.

Muriel hung up on me.

Then she called Rick's office. Brenda, the receptionist, answered the phone when Muriel called. "Mrs. Allensby, he's . . . um . . . not here."

"What do you *mean* he's not there? Is he in a meeting? Is he at lunch? I demand to speak with him AT ONCE."

"Mrs. Allensby, he's not . . . *here* . . . I don't know what to say. I'll put you through to Mr. Allensby's secretary . . . "

Jackie Miller, Rick's right hand, is a gem. "My God, Mrs. Allensby, I thought you *knew* . . . after Susan's call yesterday, he just . . . kind of keeled over and . . . it was over so suddenly . . . " Her voice broke. "It's very difficult for me to talk about, Mrs. Allensby . . . "

Muriel began mumbling to herself and hung up on Jackie.

Jackie called me and told me.

I dialed Muriel's number. She answered immediately.

"Gotcha, Muriel," I said quietly, and hung up.

After that, I had so much fun with Muriel that I almost forgot that Rick was out of town.

The day after the "Rick is dead" gotcha, a painfully young, newly married couple walked through my flower bed, walked around my house and knocked on the front door. They said that they were interested in seeing the house; while they didn't understand how I could be asking such a small price for a house its size, they were delighted with what they'd seen from the outside.

I told them I wasn't sure what they were talking about, and that the house was definitely not for sale. The young woman got upset and confused; the young man was working hard to handle the situation as best he could.

I invited them in for coffee. It didn't take long to confirm my suspicion that Muriel was behind this, and that it had flopped rather badly. She'd wanted to rattle me, and had succeeded for ten seconds, but she hadn't used friends to play Gotcha, she'd used innocent kids who didn't understand the game. They really were looking for a house. I called a realtor friend, and sent them off to meet with her. Then I got mad.

I couldn't think clearly, so I went out to the studio to focus and burn my anger out on *The Wild Mare*. I got so involved that I ended up spending the rest of the day on it. I actually did some good work, got frighteningly close to finishing it.

Exhausted but calm, I popped dinner in the microwave, poured myself some iced tea and thought. What would drive Muriel insane? Muriel is the kind of woman who could never admit that she was in an awkward position; she's the kind that would see an unpleasant situation through rather than have to admit that a major faux pas had been committed.

So what can I tell you about the fifteen Hare Krishnas that arrived at Muriel's for dinner that Monday night at my invitation? They had their books, their flowers, their babies, their incense, cymbals, drums, tambourines and chants; fifteen very loving and highly excitable people ready to share their faith and good works with Strictly Baptist Muriel Allensby, whose beloved daughter-in-law had, in strictest confidentiality, told whoever had answered the phone at the local Hare Krishna temple that Muriel had been expressing interest in the religion and wanted to meet some of them, and so wanted them to come to her home for dinner. Could a few of them be there for dinner at six?

I would have given anything to see her face when she opened the front door. I can tell you that she fed them all very well, was generous and polite and listened to what everyone had to say. I don't know how she got them to go home after dinner, or whether she's going to convert from Baptist Reality. I know for a fact, though, that she went to bed with a migraine and didn't get up for two days.

"Gotcha," I whispered into the air.

Rick kept his promise; he called me at bedtime every night. Things were going well in New York; he was keeping things going after the star architect quit the parent office in Manhattan and left the place in panicked chaos. I told him that I hadn't seen Muriel, but that we'd spoken on the telephone. He was content, and talked about New York some more before he told me how much he missed me and wished me good night.

Muriel survived her migraine as well as her adventure with the Hare Krishnas. She even managed to pull together a fairly good gotcha a day or so later.

The day before Rick was due home, I got a phone call from a production assistant from the local morning talk show. He seemed nervous but he did his job.

"You're Susan Allensby?"

I was confused, but I know who I am. "That's me."

"Ms. Allenby, I'm with the *Good Day* show. We're doing a show in three weeks about transsexuals, and your agent called and said that you've been writing a book about your crossover experiences that you'd be interested in sharing with us and our viewers. I understand that the book isn't finished and that you haven't found a publisher for it, but that's okay. We only have to mention that you've got a book in progress — who knows? Maybe it'll get enough attention from the show that you'll get a publisher!"

I was having trouble connecting. "What?"

He wasn't aware of my confusion. He'd mistaken it for shyness. Good Lord.

"It's okay, Ms. Allensby. You won't be the only transsexual on the show. And there'll be some transsexuals in the audience, so you won't feel alone. Everyone'll be telling their personal stories, and the audience will be asking questions, same format as always. You DO watch *Good Day*, don't you?"

Did I? I couldn't remember. Muriel was coming along, though, cooking stuff like this up. I was impressed. This was *good*.

"Do you have my agent's phone number?"

He rifled through some papers. "Yes, it's right here." He gave me Muriel's number, of course. "Why? Is something wrong?"

"No, not a thing. I just wanted to make sure you're on the up and up. You could just be part of a practical joke, and I don't take to those very well." I was having fun now.

The production assistant bristled. "I can assure you, Ms. Allensby, that I am calling for the *Good Day* show. If you'd like verification of that, please hang up and call the television station, ask for the show and ask to speak with me again; my name is Allan Williams."

Muriel had done better than I thought. "That won't be necessary, Mr. Williams."

He relaxed. "Between you and me, Muriel Richards said you'd be kind of hard to pin down, and that you'd turn us down right away."

He suddenly noticed that I wasn't giving him a bad time. "For what it's worth, she said you had one helluva story."

Up to this point, I didn't know what I was going to do. Then suddenly, I was seized by a blinding flash of inspiration. I was going to turn this gotcha around. Muriel would die. "I'd *love* to do the show. Just send the necessary forms, releases and recommendations to Muriel and she'll see to it that I get everything done."

There was almost an audible sigh of relief. "Thanks, Ms. Allensby," he told me. "Ms. Richards will be hearing from us."

When Muriel heard back from the *Good Day* show, she nearly had a stroke. She had to call and cancel one transsexual from the lineup. Later I watched the show. It wasn't bad; I think I could have made it better.

I decided I'd better stop spending so much time planning gotchas on Muriel; they were taking me away from my painting (was *that* a gotcha from Muriel?). Rick called the night before he was due back, and told me that he was needed for at least another week. Was I all right? Could I handle a second week without him?

I was disappointed; I had missed him. But he sounded so good, so energetic, so excited that I couldn't ask him to come home.

He told me he loved me, and promised to make it up to me. Rick keeps his promises.

Muriel decided to sell her house and move into an apartment. Rick had always said that it was better for her. "There's no reason for her to have to rattle around that big, empty house alone," he'd told me on more than one occasion. "She needs a nice little place, near all the places she likes to go."

Muriel found an apartment, put down a deposit, made arrangements to sell her house and some of the things in it, and prepared to move into the new place.

Muriel's new apartment is four blocks from our house.

Maybe I wasn't the gotcha queen after all. I had had some fun, but I had created a monster. This was the best gotcha yet — and it was on ME.

I had to think, and think fast. I couldn't block her apartment, I couldn't stop the selling of her house. Killing her was out, for now.

Rick and I could not live four blocks from Muriel. Rick is not good at defining house rules and making them stick. With Muriel this close, I was never going to have a moment's peace. Ever. There would be fighting, screaming, crying and leaving. The marriage would be over. Muriel would again take an active role in the running of Rick's life, without me in it.

I had to do something, even if it was only to buy myself a little time to think of something bigger.

I spent two full days trying to think of everyone I've ever known, friends, business contacts, people at the supermarket, old college pals — there had to be a peg I could hang my next move on. But what was it?

The next day, after I thought the plan through, I couldn't believe I'd agonized over it. It was so very simple; a little expensive, but relatively painless.

Three days later, Muriel called me in a rush of excitement. She'd received a phone call, "one of those annoying contests that nobody ever wins because the questions are so obscure," she said. "But I did it, I won!"

"What are you talking about?" She had awakened me out of a sound sleep, in which I'd been dreaming about riding *The Wild Mare* with Rick.

"The question was: 'Which Biblical character spent three days in the belly of a whale?' and I said 'Jonah' without even giving it a thought!"

Muriel knows her Bible.

"That's great, Muriel." I was still half asleep. I should have been with Rick.

"Susan, don't you want to know what I've won?"

"Sorry, Muriel, I'm still half-dozing. Tell me. What did you win?"

"You won't believe it, but I've won air fare for two to Australia! Isn't that unbelievable?"

My eyes flew open. "Muriel! Australia?"

She was very happy, happier than I'd heard her sound in years. I was suddenly glad for her. "Isn't it wonderful? I'm going to Australia!"

"I don't know, Muriel, it's awfully far away . . . "

"Don't spoil this, Susan. It's wonderful!"

I couldn't help it. It WAS wonderful. I agreed with her. "Congratulations, Muriel, I mean it."

"Normally the first person I'd think of to take with me on a trip like this is Richard," she chattered, but without the usual tinge of malice. "But he's not due back for a couple of days, right?"

"Right," I moaned. I missed him.

"Well, Susan, the one catch to this deal is that I have to leave no later than Monday morning."

"Muriel, that's only three days away! You're not all moved into your new place, and you haven't sold your house yet!"

"All that can wait. I have always wanted to go to Australia; Bill and I talked about going, and we were planning on it the year he died. Now I get to go — I'm not passing this up!"

"Hold it, Muriel, three days is not enough time to settle your affairs so you can leave for — just how long are you planning to be gone?"

"It's an open-ended ticket; I have to leave by Monday, but I can stay two weeks, three weeks, a month, even longer if I want to . . . "

"But Muriel — " I began.

"Look, Susan, I have enough money to go and have a grand time. I've asked Helen Mead to go with me. Her husband died a few years ago, and she's as ready as I am to go. So we're doing it."

"You'll never get everything in order so you can be gone by Monday, Muriel."

"I will," Muriel said quietly, "if you'll come help me."

So I helped her. We met with the realtors, I helped her organize her move, I helped her get rid of some of the junk in the house. I even went shopping with her, to get her outfitted properly for her adventure. The movers will get the last of the things she wants to keep delivered to her apartment. I'll oversee that so that Muriel has nothing to worry about. The realtors will keep an eye on the house until she gets back.

I put her and her friend Helen Mead (who is actually a nice woman, about Muriel's age, with a terrific sense of humor) on the plane to Australia. Muriel knows that they are going to have the time of their lives.

What Muriel doesn't know is that she didn't *really* win a contest. There wasn't one. I bribed my old friend Phil Narramore at one of the radio stations to call Muriel and ask her the question so she could "win" the "contest." He told me he'd had to call her five times before he could catch her at home. She was thrilled that she had won, but he told me she called the radio station's manager twice after that to make sure this wasn't a gotcha.

Phil Narramore IS the station manager, and he was happy to verify the contest for her. I now owe him a painting. He wants *The Wild Mare*, but I'm not sure I can part with her now. She and I have a history.

The plane tickets were a little expensive; fortunately, Phil didn't tell her the trip was "all expenses paid." I'd worried about that. It looks like all Muriel needed was a little push in the right direction.

But I guess I won't have to sweat over the expense of the tickets, at least, not for very long. Last night on the telephone, I told Rick the whole story, from the beginning. He laughed so hard he fell off his bed. It seems even funnier now than when it was happening.

He was in a terrific mood when he called. He was a little tentative at first, because he wasn't sure how I'd react, but he couldn't help himself.

They want him to head the Manhattan office. It means more money, a change of scenery, a new lifestyle. They want his answer within the week. He wants to go. I think I do, too.

When Muriel comes home, we'll be packing and ready to start our adventure. I think she and I will get along better than we ever have before, especially with about three thousand miles between us.

We'll invite her to spend holidays with us, a couple of weeks in the summer . . .

. . . and if she calls us too often in the evenings, I have a pretty good idea how I'm going to handle it from now on.

ROSE ANN

BY WENDY SLOTBOOM

ROSE ANN PERCY WAS FOURTEEN ON THE DAY SHE STOOD in the clearing in front of both of our homes, scowling as I took pictures of her.

Rose Ann's face was thin and always had a tight, pinched look to it. Mean and stubborn is how my dad described her, but he always said the words in amusement, or grudging admiration, as he was shaking his head.

"The kid's got her nerve," he said. "Skin as thick as a rhino's hide. Guts like a guy's. She's probably not noticing the boys at all yet . . . am I right, Patrick?" I told him I didn't know. All I knew was that as the nearest boy, the closest non-relative, and the most available all-around, Rose Ann Percy didn't notice *me*.

Rose Ann went to school ("Ah, the taming process," my dad said), riding the same bus as me and her brothers, Mitch and William. If she had any ambitions, they were passing. There was nothing that she seemed to approach with any kind of conviction, maybe because most of her energy was restless and undirected, except when it was involved with Mitch. Mitch was the same age as me, but I never felt I knew him at all.

Mitch and Rose Ann were the oldest of the Percy kids. They left home all the time, going on extended hikes through the woods that surrounded their house and ours. They packed food and scouted deer and stayed out for days during the spring, returning like bears to hibernate in the fall.

Mitch and Rose Ann slept in the living room when they were home. Their parents had one of the bedrooms and the younger kids, William and Lorli, shared the other. Mitch and Rose Ann slept fully clothed in sleeping bags arranged on the floor. Boots were kicked off and scattered nearby. While they slept, the TV sometimes stayed on all night long.

"Smile," I told Rose Ann the day I was photographing her in the clearing.

She ignored me and scuffed her way over to stand by Woody, a painted plywood woodchuck that had once stood at the edge of the parking lot of Percy's Woodchuck Lumber.

. . . .

Rose Ann was small next to the eight-foot-tall Woody. It was past the middle of October and she was dressed in warm layers of shirts, the top one blue plaid, and over it an orange down vest. The tails of the top shirt hung out from under the vest and over her jeans, and they were so long they didn't end until they were within six inches of her knees. Her jeans were faded and covered the tops of her hiking boots. The jeans used to belong to Mitch, just like everything else she was wearing.

There was no competition for Rose Ann's heart. Mitchell Joseph Percy, with his otter-sleek dark brown hair and clear gray eyes, had it all. He had a stillness and maturity that seemed rare. He was quick and kind. Knowledgeable. Gentle. They may have looked alike, but in many ways Mitch was the antithesis of Rose Ann.

"You can quit looking like that," I told Rose Ann. "You're never going to be a cover girl looking that way."

"What do *you* know," she said. Mitch would never have answered that way. He never responded with defiance. Mitch seemed above rebellion. The whole time I knew him, he went quietly his own way. Once of the few people he seemed genuinely close to was Rose Ann.

And that's what I wanted, to be close to Rose Ann. After I got my camera, I tried to persuade her that she could be a model. I don't know if she believed me or not. She studied a lot of magazines and analyzed hundreds of models' faces, bodies and clothes, but exactly what she had on her mind, as she hunched over a magazine opened out on the kitchen table, was hard for me to say.

"You're not pretty enough," her mother sometimes told her when she saw Rose Ann concentrating on those magazines, assuming, like I did, that Rose Ann's intensity was a silent declaration of some deep interest, some kind of hope that Rose Ann held for herself.

"How many pictures are left on the roll?" Rose Ann asked me. I told her seven. She was wearing her hunting cap with the earflaps down and she pushed it backed on her head until the visor was pointing forty-five degrees into the sky. She scratched her forehead where her hairline started and I got a picture as she went to pull the visor back down. "No," I told her. "Keep your hand there."

"What?" she said. "Here on my hat?"

"Yeah. And bring your elbow forward so I can see it. And then kind of tilt your head back and close your eyes."

She did it but she looked self-conscious. "This feels stupid," she said.

And it did look awkward, almost silly, but I snapped it anyway, always finding excuses for taking any picture, even bad ones, of Rose Ann.

She scowled at me and pulled her hat down firmly.

"Smile, Rose Ann," I told her, still looking at her through my camera. "Smile like I've been gone away for two years. And you've missed me and all of a sudden after two or three years I'm back. Smile how you would then."

She just looked at me. "I see you every day," she said.

"You're no fun," I told her and lowered my camera until it was hanging by the strap around my neck. She took off her hat and twirled it around on her finger a few times before putting it back on with the bill in the back. Then she buried her hands in the pockets of her down vest.

"You know," I said. "Maybe you'd be better at this if you had the right clothes."

Rose Ann looked at me and then ignored me.

"Yeah, I bet you would," I said, "but you *don't* have the right clothes. You just have Mitch's clothes."

She hesitated for a minute. "So?"

"So, you look stupid."

Rose Ann turned on her heel and started heading across the clearing to her front door.

"Wait," I called after her and I hurried a few steps to catch up. "Are you mad?"

She didn't look at me this time, or answer, and I followed her into the kitchen of her house. We wiped our feet on a mat inside the door before stepping onto the scuffed white tile. The Percys had this kind of floor in their entire house except for a few spots where it was covered with a little mat or some kind of rug or deerhide.

Rose Ann went to the stove and while I sat down at the kitchen table she stuck her finger in a pan of coffee to see if it was warm.

"I heard Mitch and your dad and my dad all talking about the hunt before they left this morning," I told Rose Ann when she brought her coffee over. I was baiting her into talking to me. She always had a fearful attitude when Mitch went on a hunt without her. She became nervous and withdrawn, and even less sociable than usual.

Rose Ann sat down and pulled up her feet so they hung by the bootheels off the rungs of her chair.

"They're hunting off the Scully Fork, I think."

"Oh yeah?" She swallowed some coffee. "That's nothing surprising." She wrapped her hands around her mug and bent over and looked into her coffee like she was examining it.

I remembered riding with them in the pickup truck, Mitch driving, a deer (Rose Ann had shot) in the back. Everyone was away from home when we drove in. Rose Ann and Mitch pulled the deer from the truck onto the ground and dressed him in the clearing. Mitch held the deer on his back, untied his hind legs and told Rose Ann in his quiet voice what to do. And, following his instructions, Rose Ann edged her knife into the deer and slid her hand in under the skin.

As I watched her hand, a current shot from my groin to my chest to my face. I felt like I had twice the usual amount of blood in my body, and all of it had centered in the places where I was most likely to feel its heat.

"You should know," I told Rose Ann, returning to her comment.

At that moment Mrs. Percy came into the kitchen steering Rose Ann's four-year-old sister Laurel Lee in front of her.

"I'm going to be gone for a while, Rose Ann," she said. "I'm leaving Lorli with you." She gave Lorli a push and Lorli ran over behind Rose Ann and started to throw her weight against the back of Rose Ann's chair.

"Knock it off, Lorli," Rose Ann said. "Come around here." Mrs. Percy was gone and Lorli was still butting up against Rose Ann's chair.

"Why?" Lorli said.

"Because I want you to stop knocking into my chair," Rose Ann told her.

Lorli giggled. "Why?" She climbed onto the back rungs of the chair and hung onto the top. Rose Ann had been sitting forward in the chair, just on the edge of it, and when she stood up the chair was pulled over by Lorli's weight. Lorli hung onto the chair the whole time it was falling. She landed on her back and hit her head on the floor. The chair fell on top of her and she started to cry.

"That's why," Rose Ann said, as she pulled the chair off Lorli and sat it upright. "You're not supposed to bang into chairs or climb on them, you're supposed to sit on them. You're not hurt," she added and stood Lorli up just like she had the chair. "Who's tough, Laurel Lee?" Lorli was wiping at her tears. "Hey Lorli, who's a tough one?"

"*I* am," Lorli said.

"Yeah," Rose Ann answered. "That's right." She sat down sideways in the chair with her shoulders slumped forward a little and her arm hanging over the back of the chair. Her profile was turned to me and her hat was still backwards on her head.

"Why are you worrying about Mitch?" I asked her. "He's probably glad to be with someone else for a change. You ever think he might get sick of you always hanging around him? He's two years older than you, you know. He's *my* age."

Rose Ann watched Lorli clean up her face with her sleeve and then pull a bag of cookies off a countertop. As the cookies spilled onto the floor, Lorli picked up one in each fist and stared at them, deciding which to eat first.

"Nothing's going to happen to Mitch," I told Rose Ann impatiently.

And then Rose Ann turned and looked at me like she already knew I was going to be proven wrong.

I wasn't there when Rose Ann got the phone call from her father. Her mother was still gone; Rose Ann was still babysitting Lorli in her own haphazard way. The hunting trip had run overtime. Mr. Percy, my dad and William had spent two hours searching for Mitch. They had shouted for him, but he didn't answer their calls. When they found him he was dead, killed by a drunken hunter who had mistaken him for a deer and then deserted him when he discovered his error.

I couldn't get close to Rose Ann for a week after it happened. At the funeral she was silent. Her eyes had a stricken look that I couldn't face. At school, whenever she saw me, she would turn and walk away.

Finally, with my camera around my neck for security, I went to her house and knocked on the door. She answered it and stood staring at me. She was dressed from head to toe in Mitch's clothes.

It was no different than the way she had dressed for years, but with Mitch dead it scared me.

Rose Ann waited for me to speak but I couldn't think of anything to say. She focused on my camera. "I'm not going to be a model," she told me, "So you can just go away." She gave the door a push and I watched it swing toward me and shut between us. I still hadn't said one word to Rose Ann.

William says that Rose Ann has cut her hair. It's now as short as Mitch's had been.

"Mitch?" her dad says, confused, "Mitch?"

And Lorli, happy to know the right answer for once, pipes up and says, "Daddy, that's *Rose Ann.*"

MOUNTAIN MAN

BY VALERIE A. LEAF

I FIRST MET JACK IN THE SPRING OF 1973 AT THE LOCAL watering hole, where I worked as a bartender. It became immediately apparent he had long since abandoned any wish for material gain and seemed well entrenched in a lifestyle that revolved mostly around living off the land in particularly innovative ways. He was thirty-five, a little rough around the edges, bearded, and residually handsome, I thought, often imagining how he would look clean-shaven and in a business suit.

I was twenty-one, had just quit college after a memorable trip to Europe, and was ready for adventure in the Idaho ski resort. He didn't believe me when I told him I could play softball with the best of them, and that, thanks to my older brother, I didn't throw like a girl.

He leaned over the bar, as if in confidence, and spoke softly. "Now look here, then — we'll see what you're made of; you come out to the playfield tomorrow, rain or shine, and I'll see if you've got the stuff to be on my team. Bring your glove and don't wear high heels. I'll be workin' you hard."

I passed muster with him that spring; thus began a most memorable softball season. "Woman, you've got to run like the wind around the bases. If you were a duck, you'd be dead in the water. Stride out, dig in, ain't nobody should be faster than you," he chided.

My girlhood had included pickup baseball games with my brother and his friends, but I had never had a coach before. It was exhilarating to be caught up in the spirit of the game with Jack, who appreciated my athletic ability and pushed me to do better. After a good hit, he'd widen his eyes and clap his hands. "Hee, hee, now you got it."

During one particular playoff game at the end of that first season, we were leading by one run in the top of the seventh inning with two outs. The opponents had runners on first and second with their best hitter up. I was playing deep in center field when a solid line drive was hit between the right fielder and me. Anticipating its velocity, I chased it up on the first bounce, turned and threw it as hard as I could to our waiting third baseman, who nailed the runner as the ball sailed in low on one bounce. Three outs, one run scored, and the game was tied.

Before I had time to get excited by my feat, Jack was running out to center field, whooping and jumping with glee as our team hustled in. He caught me up in a crushing embrace. "Way to throw, Woman! That was magnificent," he beamed.

My line-drive home run down the right field line clinched our championship. He bragged the story around town and for days afterward I was congratulated by friends and strangers alike.

As the summer wore on in our small mountain town, Jack would drop by the bar and plant himself upright on the end stool to observe the comings and goings. Hunting cap pulled down low, chewing on a toothpick, he would amuse himself by watching me pour drinks, occasionally chuckling to himself and interjecting a wry remark to no one in particular. He always ordered Jack Daniels neat. "Now don't go ruinin' good whiskey with all the ice and sugared mixers. If you're brave, you can come up to my place and I'll let you sample some home brew that will curl your toes." He saw me stiffen. "Now don't you be scared of me. I'm a gentleman under these muddy clothes. Ain't been to no finishing school, but make no mistake, I know how to treat a lady right." Somehow, I believed him.

"Are you saying I'm a *lady* then?" I asked bemusedly.

"You bet, darlin'," he assured me. It was a compliment and hinted at a world of romance, a world that my tomboyish childhood had made seem impossibly remote and far into the future.

It became a game of wits replete with nuance and innuendo. Jack would come to my cottage and dare me to cook something without opening a can. "Woman, do you know how to skin a hare and cook it over an open fire? I don't want meat that's been sitting around in plastic wrap and styrofoam."

One day, he surprised me with a gift, *The Joy of Cooking*. I couldn't picture him browsing in a bookstore and choosing such a book. Only later did I realize it had been signed by his mother: "To Jack, since you never come home for my cooking anymore."

After softball season ended, I saw Jack mostly at a distance, driving around town with various loads in his huge flatbed pickup with removable slats. Sometimes he'd have cut wood, a load of cacophonous chickens, even a mule loaded down with pickaxes for gold mining. He wouldn't use a phone but would drop notes by my door.

To Monica
Latitude 48, looking east

Come let me show you where the wild onions grow —
where the blueberries hang lush on the vine at the
stream's edge, where a day's worth of fishing will feed us
for a month, where a man like me can explain things
you might not understand. I'll come calling the first
light of dawn and if you can see your way clear to grace
me with your shining presence, I think we might find
something in common.

On our drive up through the foothills of the Sawtooths, the thin
sunlight of October and the trees shedding their summer verdure lent a
view of stark vistas across the gently sloping hills sprinkled with aspens.
We drove north of town, bumping and creaking and listening to the
truck's engine protesting the rarefied mountain air.

As we turned off on the narrow dirt road, Jack pointed to the sky.
"Now look there. You see those birds flyin' south? It's early for that.
Means we'll be seeing plenty of snow up here. Got to bring the sheep to
lower ground soon. You in with me, Partner? It's a far sight easier than
rustlin' cattle," he teased.

We arrived at his cabin in good time and sat on the porch in the
midday sun, eating the dried venison and squaw bread he had made in
his iron skillet.

"This is all a man really needs to be happy. Those new kitchen
gadgets don't do a thing but make food so you can't recognize it." He
paused, waiting for me to defend my right to own a blender. "Same as
that face paint you wear. I could feed a Hopi Indian for a year on what
you spend to attract men. Your face don't need it, Darlin'. Won't save
you from a bear in the woods," he warned.

I asked him about the skins he had drying on a line that stretched
from the porch out to an evergreen. "Elk," he replied. "Nothin' more
tender 'cept maybe a baby's bottom — or yours," he added with a
devilish grin. He easily ducked my arm as I swiped at him.

"You don't know anything about my bottom," I retorted.

"Not yet, but I'm a patient man," he said quietly as he picked up my hand. "Now quit your sassing for a minute. Takin' into account that you are sweet on me even if you're fightin' it, my reckoning is we could have some fine children to grow up and see after our bones when we're worn out. Good times we'll have and you can get on down to see your folks when the weather's fine and I'll tend to the garden and the animals. You'll get your fill of the citified life, just like I did, and you'll be longing for the crisp air and trees blowin' in the wind."

His reverie made me fidgety with its uncharacteristically serious tone. "Jack, I . . . my life is just starting . . . and I've just begun to explore the world. It's . . . can't we be friends like before?" It sounded weak and my voice trailed off.

He reached over and embraced me, propping my chin up with his roughened hand. "Now, before you go sayin' no, I'm gonna kiss you so you know you been kissed." And he did, and I did. He felt some of the fight drain out of me.

"You go on out into the world and pretty soon you'll be wondering if everyone ain't half mad to be knocking themselves dead and getting nowhere. And for what? A little pocket change and flowers in the window? Can't feed a family harvesting pansies, can you? Now as far as I can see, only thing missin' here is a good woman like you. I'd take real good care of you."

Fall gave way to early snows and the crush of excited skiers on holiday. Jack didn't come to the bar that winter.

But his note said, "Red flag planted in the snow at the turnoff. Fire and warm heart waiting."

IN THE GALAXY OF BOUNTIFUL DREAMERS

BY NANCY BARTLEY

AS ED DOVE, FIFTY-THREE, DESCRIBES IT, HE WAS IN THE conservatory of the Gospel Mission when the spaceship landed. He gazed up and saw a white light radiating from the black, frozen heaven beyond the window, lifted his arms and cried: "You've come for me at last! You didn't forget me!"

"We never forgot you, Ed," Capt. Harmon Glitza replied. "Why, we've been monitoring you for years."

"Then they used levitation on me and took me up to the ship for dinner," Ed says. "Then the captain beamed me back down into the conservatory. He had to go. He was catching a fishing charter."

I lean back in my chair and smile, tapping my pencil against my chin. Ed is off his Thorazine again and his face is flushed with the eagerness of a child witnessing the miracle of Christmas — a child who discovers that Santa does exist, that there is a star guiding us to Bethlehem. In Ed's case it is a spaceship.

"You see, I came to this planet when I was just a kid," Ed says eagerly. His gnarled hands are folded in his lap and his eyes are wide — twin horizons of electric blue — in a wizened face. "The captain brought me here and set me down in the front yard of the Dove family of Spokane, Washington, because the schools are better than on Rommelspore."

"Rommelspore?" I ask.

"The Planet Rommelspore in the solar system of Hellatrix in the constellation of Capricorn," he says.

"Oh, *that* Rommelspore," I reply, shifting my position so I can meet him eye to eye.

"It's the one and only. You should go there sometime," he says.

"Maybe next year. I haven't any vacation left. Ed, have you been taking your medication?" I ask. He shuffles his feet like a kid and shrinks into the chair.

"I can't. They'll take control of me," he says. The eyes are apprehensive. Ed grew up in the state mental health system, until, at the age of fifty, he was released in the name of deinstitutionalization. I hate being the voice of reality when he seems happy on Rommelspore.

"Who takes control of you?" I ask, my pencil poised and ready to resume taking notes.

"Katie Barnes and the Preacher," he says. "They make me do things. They won't let the captain come for me."

"Well, Ed, it's up to you. But you should follow the doctor's orders," I say. What the hell, it's what I'm supposed to say. I know he's crazy. I know the plain, brick building with the "Happy Birthday Jesus" sign in the window needs all the room possible just for cots for street folks like Ed — not for a hoity-toity conservatory for growing fragile plants. I know, too, that Katie Barnes who runs the place is a saint and that old Preacher, who stands in the park warning of the coming of Armageddon, is just as crazy as Ed and probably as harmless.

I want to tell Ed to chuck the tranquilizer that turns him listless and unfeeling and go ahead and talk to the captain, fly to Rommelspore. It has to be better than the reality of sleeping at the mission or freezing under the pavilion in the park in one of Seattle's coldest winters on record.

"Mike, do you know what it's like to talk to the stars?" he asks.

He talks to me of these things because I have three letters behind my name — Michael Marshall, MSW — and that puts me in this cracked green Naugahyde chair at this metal desk in this nicotine-stained office called Community Mental Health on Seattle's skid row, a narrow part of town tightly hemmed with boutiques, restaurants, and galleries. It puts me here listening and Ed — and the many, many others like him that wander in or are referred by the mission or the hospital up the hill — on the stained brown sofa, confiding.

My wife, Chris, says there is an opening for a social worker in an office not far from the school in Bellevue where she teaches French. I say, "That's nice," and turn the pages of the sports section. Sometimes I think of that job in a private clinic. We could move to that three-bedroom, Phinney Ridge bungalow Chris loves, the one with the breakfast nook, big roomy kitchen and flower boxes. I know I should apply for the job. Living out one's fantasy is not always profitable. The truth is, I love it here among the dregs because I'm one of them, son of a no-account, seldom-employed laborer and a too-fragile mother, who together created their own realities through gin. I'm carved from the rudiments of life experience, tempered only by the refinement of higher education. God bless the G.I. Bill.

I work here because I am a selfish man who takes private pleasure in small victories: Ed's trust when he mistrusts the rest of the world; Bountiful Washington's slight smile and even her tears after a lifetime of emotional drought; Preacher's hail from the park bench, "The Lord is coming, Brother Mike!"

Among them, I stand strong and tall. It's easy to quarterback their team, easy as long as you accept that the victories will be small.

When I met Bountiful she was in the Harborview emergency room, with slashes across both wrists. The doc was stitching her up but she never made a sound. She is a beautiful and fragile woman with skin smooth like polished mahogany. She came to my office twice and sat quietly staring at her slender hands. "I'm a model, you know," she says, gazing up at me beneath velvet lashes. "Tell me about it," I say.

"Someday I'm going to go to New York. Someday I'm going to be somebody."

She disappeared for six months, but just the other day I saw her again, a violet sweater tight over her curvy body, long legs ending somewhere beneath a small, red-leather skirt. I call to her and motion for her to follow me inside the Grand Central Arcade and out of the rain. Her eyes dart about suspiciously. She is trembling from the cold. "So it's you, Doctor. What do you want?"

"No, I'm not a doctor," I reply. "Do you have a minute?"

"What do you want?" she repeats. "You're going to make me late for an appointment."

"Let me buy you something to eat, just a minute," I urge.

"I don't need anything to eat. I just had this big lunch with a client. Took me way up there to the top of that building," she says, pointing to the SeaFirst Building with its famed French restaurant at the top. Nevertheless, she follows me inside. I buy her a croissant and cappuccino and we sit by the fireplace.

She eats ravenously, takes her shoes off and places them on the hearth. The soft breath of the gas-fed fire mingles with the trickling notes of piano music. Our faces reflect in a blaze of gold ornaments — long distorted faces swimming as the ornaments turn on the red-bow-decked tree, among a galaxy of little stars. Little Rommelspores, I muse.

The classic arcade is filled with closing sounds, the slam of bakery gates, the click of heels across brick, the hush of traffic passing through rain turned to sleet. She sips from her steaming mug, eyes running over the

Italian leather shoes in the shop window, the gleam of art deco jewelry in the showcase.

"I'm going to model that stuff for those people who own the store," she says, indicating the display case. "I'm working on a deal right now."

"Bountiful, how old are you?" I ask gently. She refused to tell anyone her age that night at the hospital. I guessed it to be about eighteen. I'd heard she'd been living off the streets for three or four years.

"What's my age to you?" she snaps. "You interested in my price?"

"I care. I'm just concerned for you. I haven't seen you around for a while and after the night I met you at Harborview — well, I was worried about you."

"I don't need you and I don't need this." She shoves the mug across the table in my direction. "Who do you think you are? I mean who the hell do you think you are?" I've pulled her from her world and into mine.

"Okay. Okay," I say, trying to calm her. I've gone too far.

"You call me in here and butt into my life and ask all kinds of questions and next thing you know you'll be telling me to quit the business and get a job at Woolworth."

"No. That's your decision," I say.

"You bet it is. I like what I do. I'm a model. I'm a high class model. Men pay . . . someday I'm going to New York. I'm going to be somebody and no two-cent shrink like you is going to tell me any different!"

For a moment, I see the eyes glisten. I want to run my thumb down her forehead and tell her it's good-dream magic, like I do when my daughter Jenny is afraid of nightmares. I want to create another history for her and a new future.

"I'm sorry. I'm sorry," I say. I admit, I'm obsessed with what might happen to her out there alone. I try to stop her, but she jerks her arm free and for a moment our eyes lock and I can say no more. Although I want to punch through her illusions, I cannot voice my fear and shatter the myth she wraps around herself. It's all she has. I watch as she disappears into the twilight.

Bountiful Washington, a sum of poor women's illusions and faint dreams. Sometimes it seems my job is to shatter those illusions and strip them of even the shallow joys they have.

Ed and his spaceships, Bountiful and her modeling career, Preacher and his avenging messiah, bringing justice with lightning and fire, perhaps the best gift I can give them is respect for the illusions they choose. But at what price, I ask myself. It is painful to see Bountiful go out into the streets, to risk her life in some third-floor seedy hotel room.

I saw her once purr against the body of some slick dude in studded leather. Ever since she's been in and out of my dreams — not one woman, but many copies of her, as many as there are stars, staring, lifeless, with frozen faces, small slits at the wrists. As I walk among the galaxy, streams of red lacquer pool at my feet. I shout something and wake up to find Chris leaning over me.

"You've had that dream again," she says, patting my shoulder and then rolling over to face the wall. "Just a dream," she murmurs. There are times when I need good-dream magic.

Even so, I love my work. Chris doesn't understand why. Such tragedy, such need, she says. How can you work in it day after day?

Chris speaks French, teaches young women at St. Thomas Aquinas Academy for Girls. She lives French. Each night for the last three weeks her small hands have clasped a faded blue volume of short stories — Zola, de Maupassant, even Colette. I watch her read. She is immersed in another world, one of silken, satin rustling coverlets and curtains, of blue boudoirs and countrysides with rambling lanes, ancient vineyards, meadows and quaint cottages.

My wife is like a dazzling and mysterious gift, layer after layer of complex and intriguingly beautiful wrapping and I'm still unsure what is at the core. It is that mystery I find both frightening and appealing, that tenuous connection with something glittering and beautiful, descended from the heavens right within my reach. She offers a world as far from my own as if it were encased in glass — a spun-glass ornament I hold gently between clumsy hands — a place I can never enter.

We met in college. She was a serious student, a French major, daughter of a bank executive who drank himself to death on J&B scotch. We dated just a short time when I asked her to marry me. I had to move fast. I didn't want her to get away. No one was more surprised than I when she said yes. After all, I was just a working guy, an average student, an ordinary man in a plain brown wrapper. There are no surprises.

Chris met me for lunch the other day, gliding into this office fragrant as flowers, a cloud of spring in December, all wrapped up in her blue cap and coat the color of her eyes. She hugs her coat to her, looks around the office quickly — butterfly glances — and then says, "About ready? I'll wait outside."

I suggest we walk and she feeds the meter where her practical Honda Civic waits. I want her to see me in my world as I see her — all swathed in mysterious French — in hers. She takes my arm as we stroll through the park where Preacher rails. Ed sits in a pale pool of December sunlight, smiling, waiting for his spaceship to pierce through the frigid air.

A Christmas concert in Occidental Square has just concluded and in place of well-heeled shoppers reveling in the holiday spirit, the white plastic chairs — rigid as tombstones and stamped with "Property of City of Seattle" — are filled with decaying men and women. The eyes of a gaunt, old, blind woman beam a challenge to the heavens. On her coat Preacher has pinned a "Praise the Lord" button. She rocks herself and swears as he storms and speaks of wrath and saving grace. "Come now. Come now, oh, long-awaited Messiah! Smite the evil from their hearts," he calls to the blank clouds.

A young mother with tangled hair strums a guitar and sings in a faint, strained voice. She gazes over the heads of the crowd around her, rocking to the rhythm, a coatless toddler motionless in a pack on her back. Wind ruffles the baby's blond curls. For a moment I wonder if the child is dead.

"Do something!" Chris whispers. She looks up at me, her eyes full of tears. Chris seldom cries. I reach for my wallet and place five dollars in the guitar case. Along a wall, someone had scrawled, "Pimps Stole the Sun."

Chris turns her head toward the boutique across the street. I force myself not to think of how she probably hasn't been inside one in a long time. "Let's go, please," she implores. I lead my wife past the pawnshops and peep shows down to the market and her favorite French café, one of her few luxuries.

We live near Beacon Hill, in a plain, three-bedroom rambler we share with our daughter Jenny and my black lab, Gus. We've been burglarized twice. The last time, they took Chris' grandmother's wedding ring and Jenny's silver baby spoon, shattered the frame of our wedding photo and stole the best of our clothes. They didn't bother with our old black-and-white TV with the bent rabbit ears.

"The place is affordable," I tell Chris. "That's all it is," she adds. Times like that are when I buy her flowers or a piece of old, embroidered linen or something. Once I treated her to a play because it had "Paris" in the title. That's all it took and she was off in her own world again, somewhere I have never traveled. It seems she can stand anything as long as she has her books, her keepsakes — and Jenny — around her.

It's not the best neighborhood, I'll admit. But after all these years, it's familiar, an extension of my daily life. It's like the turf where I grew up, and for Chris, anywhere we live still wouldn't be France. Anywhere, her world would be separate from mine.

To me, French is a language invented to make fools of American men. I don't try to pronounce the words, but when I found the book, *French Bedtime Stories*, all dusty and dog-eared in a used bookstore near my office, I knew Chris must have it. She almost cried when I gave it to her and threw her arms around my neck. She liked it more than the vacuum cleaner I bought her last Christmas. She cried then, too.

Chris, whose grandfather came from Sweden, began teaching Jenny French before our daughter could walk. I asked, "Why not Swedish?" and she replied it was a cold and passionless language. I do not remind her of her roots that made her seek refuge in books.

Jenny believes her own heritage to be French. She converses easily with her mother, soft volleys of vowel sounds that play above the drone of the game I am watching in the living room. A siren screams through the neighborhood so I turn up the TV volume until it's passed.

In a moment I hear the phone ring, hear Chris speak. The door swings shut, but still I can hear her voice. Someone from her school has called. "My husband? Right, a psychologist," she says. I hear her speak of my "practice" and my "patients."

I've given up correcting her. I'm no Ph.D. It annoys me that she tells those lies. Just like her mother taught her, "Appearance is everything." Hell, I feel like a kid in an oversized suit, trying to be something I'm not.

All those lofty things Chris learned about family name and impression as her father — sober nine to five — stumbled drunk and crying through the house each night, a fool in a pinstripe suit.

"My mother should have left him!" Chris said one time, in an uncharacteristic burst of rage.

"Why?" I demanded. "He needed her. Maybe the bottle was all he had. Do you throw in the towel because someone isn't giving you the lifestyle you want? Can't he be weak? Isn't he allowed to fail without losing all?" My own anger shocked me and we stared at each other for moments. Then her tears came and I drew her into the circle of my arms.

The door to the kitchen, where Chris and Jenny sit conspiring, is still shut. All I hear is the babble of the announcer speculating on the quarterback's hamstrings and the cheerful ditty of a beer ad. Gus thumps his tail and gazes at me with dog-eyed adoration that almost makes me squirm.

"How are you doing, Old Geezer?" I ask, scratching his ears. He grovels with delight and his tail slaps at a low-hanging bough of the Christmas tree. Chris and Jenny decorated the tree with porcelain dolls in taffeta and stiff lace caps: gilded braid and teal-blue satin balls and blown-glass snowflakes revolve slowly, capturing rays of blue and rose light, swirling colors, remnants of Chris's childhood. Sometime later there is a wonderful sugary aroma from the kitchen. I go to the door and push it open gently. Jenny is wearing her mother's embroidered apron that hangs to her knees.

She is covered with flour and cutting cookies out of dough. Chris's back is to me. She is pulling another tray from the oven, her blond hair caught in a loose knot, exposing her ivory neck. They are singing *Il est Né*. I back away quietly. I don't want to intrude and shatter this moment. I want to remember this scene always, the epitome of awe and wonder I have for my wife. I want to remember this as I sit in the cracked green Naugahyde chair at my desk, gaze into Bountiful's sad face, Ed's electrified stare, the blue shadows beneath Preacher's eyes.

It was Christmas Eve when Katie at the mission called to say she hadn't seen Ed for more than a week. "We had words of sorts," she says. "He told me he wouldn't eat because I was putting drugs into his food that controlled his mind. I told him that was crazy."

I call the other shelters, but no Ed. I call Western State Hospital, where he spent so much of his life, but they hadn't seen him either. Late in the afternoon on Christmas Eve, Harborview Medical Center calls. Someone asks why I didn't report it when Ed stopping taking his meds. I can't answer. Ed's in intensive care, suffering from hypothermia and advanced pneumonia. He's in critical condition. Someone has written "no code" on his chart. The decision has been made to let Ed slip quietly into death as easily as he could slip into the darkness of a summer night, lie beneath it waiting for the voices of stars.

Steam hisses through the radiators. I hear the underwater murmur of nurses' voices outside the door and the slap, slap, slap of their utilitarian shoes down the long hallway.

"How are you doing, partner?" I ask gently, taking his hand.

His eyes open and he stares at me without focusing. His skin is violet as the winter twilight.

"Hello Captain," he says. "You always were my hero."

In talking to him of his childhood there had been times when I'd see the fog clear and there would be a keen view straight to his heart. Now at his bedside the clear vision I have is through his eyes, seeing only the stars beyond the window, over the glowing neon signs and strings of streetlights, over the men and women sleeping beneath the viaduct, sleeping in doorways and, as Ed had, sleeping in cardboard boxes where the rats scurry.

On the monitor I watch the weak pulsing of his heart slow, an irregular, thin green line his final voice.

Was I wrong not to insist he resume medication, call the medical authorities, have him incarcerated to protect him from himself? What kind of captain am I to allow a man to die? Is Ed happy now in the outer galaxy of imagination?

Although I want to, I don't believe in miracles. The only miracles are the gifts we give each other, that acceptance of the face we show to the world, the acquiescence to the chosen lonely course and the willingness to let the traveler go, try to make gentle bridges of caring between our worlds, to be there, if possible, when the price of illusion is paid.

It is after nine on Christmas Eve. I was supposed to be home at six. I work late every night. I want to believe I will make this up to Chris, but I know I won't and I know that, too, has its price. It is this price I fear.

I want to give so much to her. But what can I give to someone so complete? Someone I worship? I enter the quiet house. Jenny has fallen asleep beside the door to the furnace. She has hung her stocking from the doorknob — the closest thing we have to a mantel — even though she knows there really isn't a Santa Claus. But she chooses to believe. I pick her up and carry her to bed, kissing her and rubbing my thumb against her forehead and whispering, "Good-dream magic."

Chris has heard me come in and is in the kitchen ladling a bowl of onion soup, topping it with thick slices of bread, sprinkled with parmesan cheese, a Christmas Eve tradition she started.

She is barefoot, wearing a loose, silky white gown that falls softly as a snowdrift against her gentle curves. It looks vaguely like filmy curtains that used to be in Jenny's room. I sit at the table Chris has covered with her grandmother's embroidered linen cloth and watch as she twists the top from a bottle of red wine. Flames from red candles illuminate her gold wedding band, reflecting my face.

I am that which is reflected back from all of them. Layer by layer we build the fictions of our lives, each a step farther from our basest beginnings, our infantile desires. I fear the illusion of myself will be stripped away and once again I will be the small kid who dreamed of spaceships and intergalactic armor, among and yet separate from the anguish from where I came. Who would I be in Chris' world?

I worry that someday some man speaking softly will slip from the pages of her book and carry my wife away, that I will be left alone and dreamless. I want to tell her I'm sorry, sorry for not being someone else. Instead, I tell her about Ed, about his final hours. I see my image mirrored in the dark pupils of her eyes. How thin are illusions when someone we love knows the truth.

She listens intently, holding the stem of her glass between her fingers, slowly swirling the ruby wine. "I'm proud of you," she says softly.

At midnight she shuts off the light and the pale blue of our bedroom fades into murmuring darkness and the sweetness of her scent. She slides into my arms, her hair loose about her shoulders. I stroke her silky curves and speak to her of faraway places where the grapes are ripe and small lanes ramble past country cottages. Outside I hear traffic, a distant siren, the angry accusing voice of a sobbing woman. I close my eyes.

CLEO'S BARGE

BY VICTOR BOBB

IT IS QUITE A WHILE TILL FULL DARK, BUT ALREADY THERE is a transparent pale blue along the horizon which means that night is sneaking up the far side of the mountain. The hills have become black, the backlit ridges serrated by their fur of angular tamaracks and cedars. The swallows have been stitching the lake's shores together all evening, and now some of the flickering shapes flit with a jerkier motion. Bats.

"Look there." Dick points astern and to the left. A spreading ring shows where a fish has risen. Pretty good odds it's a bass, in this part of the lake. Dick remembers twenty-seven years ago when the man with him hooked what must have been five pounds of bass, but was laughing so hard at some ongoing idiocy that he lowered his rod tip and watched the line go slack, sending the fish back to whatever amused bass in those days. He has pointed to four rises in as many minutes; the figure in the back of the boat doesn't turn or say anything.

The figure's name is Dick, too. Awkward, but one of those things which happens. The only other person who might be in this boat with Dick would be Rick; and not only would Rick-and-Dick be almost as ludicrous as Dick 'n' Dick, but Dick can't stand the sonofabitch, and would probably have drowned him about eight hours and fifty rising bass ago.

He rows languidly, motionless and placid between mild-mannered pulls on the oars. When the blades come out of the water you can see that someone has painted shark teeth on them. The boat is a flat-bottomed aluminum pram twelve feet long. Long ago it was dark green, but the paint has been chipped and scratched and banged until it looks like a camouflage design. Or leprosy, or the mold that grows on the face of a corpse. The lake is still and the boat makes only a tiny swishing as they slide north along the eastern shore. A faraway coyote tries an early wail, but quiets after two unanswered cries.

"Remember the first year me and you and Jim Ed and Kerrigan were here, and Kerrigan thought the coyotes were wolves and were gonna chow down on us in our sleeping bags?" Kerrigan had been the only one of their circle with an urban background. He chuckles quietly. If the man in the stern of the rowboat makes any reply, it is not audible. Dick has paused with the oars raised. The stream of water tinkling from the blades slows to a trickle, then to drops. The boat slips almost imperceptibly along. Before he dips for another stroke, the oars have quit dripping. "Or when the Q was eating onion sandwiches, or the morning the grackles ate our breakfast?" His laugh is more than a chuckle now; full, rich and genuine. The four of them had crept down the hill to watch a merganser with her eight offspring, and when they got back, a half-dozen blackbirds were finishing off their scrambled eggs. There is another tone in the background of his laugh, perhaps a whisper of melancholy.

It is a fair-sized lake, probably two hundred ragged-edged acres, and there is no other boat visible at this end of the main arm. Perhaps it is too late in the year. Perhaps it is just fortunate chance. The shore turns suddenly eastward into a shallow bay fringed by heavy brush and some deciduous trees. Dick pulls the boat along a steady thirty feet from the bank, the quiet dip-swish dip-swish the only sound in their world. Dip-swish dip-swish dripdripdrip dripdrip drip drip . . . drip . . . d-r-i-p . . . .

Dick's voice goes very quiet, like an undertaker in the middle of a funeral telling his assistant to kill a fly. "There's not a single goddam piece of my life — seventy-three years — as good as those trips with you clowns." His face tightens and his eyes drift out of focus. His companion says nothing.

The darkness is seeping into this hollow among the mountains as though it were rising from the lake. Already it is impossible to distinguish detail on the opposite shore, a quarter mile off. The top of the hillside along which he is rowing is still well-lit.

A big fish hawk is sitting on the spar of a dead fir a hundred yards up the slope. Earlier in the year there would have been babies, squalling little birds ravenous in a jumble of sticks atop some piling or snag. Now, Dick supposes, the nest is empty and the bird has nothing to think about except whatever it is that interests him from his perch. Food, probably. Or does an old bird get thoughtful? Reflective.

Food, probably.

"*Ubi sunt* the crappie of yesteryear," Dick says. A snort of laughter floats up from the boat. They had been literate men, professors, in fact, and their corner of the lake had rippled to some pretty esoteric wisecracks at one time or another. "Nutless in Gaza." Another snort. "I heard a fly buzz when I died" — this warbled to the tune of *Yellow Rose of Texas*. Almost all Emily Dickinson would be sung to that tune, or to *A Mighty Fortress Is Our God*. These hills had many times heard ludicrous song.

Dick in the stern has shifted his weight, seems almost to be slumping sideways. "Be careful, you weenoid fag. This barge you sit in, like a burnish'd throne, burns on the water, jerk. You fall out and I'll feed you to the carp. And the grackles." The laughter is hearty again. The quote is Shakespeare, but they never had to do citations. It was just a part of their lives which they shared, like the lake or the beer and the cigars by the fire in the long slow sweet evenings.

He pulls slowly along the swoop of the bay. Just before the crescent comes to its point he lets the oars go. They bump gently against the sides of the boat. The nose slews slightly out of line and the whole boat sideslips like a ponderous skate on bad ice. Dick's forearms are on his knees and he is gazing sightlessly at the fading swirl left by the oar.

The big log has been gone for twenty or more years, but this is where it had been when they first began coming to this lake. They had anchored here, or hovered here, their poppers and their flies and Jim Ed's much-maligned artificial worms doing the various dances around the snag, up under the brush along the bank, out (rather pointlessly, usually) into the deeper part of the lake. They had sung and laughed and hooted and once when the Q was talking about his dog there had been tears. Now the boat settles as awkwardly as age seeping into joints and Dick stares into their pasts, a single muted creak and bump from one of the oars the only sound. The man in the back of the boat is stiff and quiet and does not look happy.

Bud had gone down early, dead at forty-two in his driveway; but after that they had all hung on. Till two years ago, and then it was whang whang whang, thump thump thump like a bough full of apples hitting the grass in a breeze. Jim Ed, the Q, Kerrigan, Grautz — bang, bang, bang, bang. Now there is nobody left but Dick.

He sat for a long time by the log which wasn't there watching the little flex and swirl of the placid water. There was a funny kind of yellow-green cast to this lake, but now it was too dark to see anything like that.

The little bay was the last one. The big circuit was over now. He pulled around the point, rowing steadily but without haste. There was a tiny chop out here, and the boat slapped through the water with a series of hollow plonks, like a cox beating time.

There was a light at the end of the dock. The cool nights had already begun and there weren't the midsummer swarms of bugs in the blaze of the light. He didn't have to look over his shoulder till it was time for final maneuvering. He knew when he was getting close by the pincers of light which crawled along the ripples to embrace the boat.

There was a thick-bodied woman in a plaid flannel shirt buttoning up the cover on an eighteen-foot motor boat. He shipped his left oar and heard the familiar hollow boom as the rowboat bunked gently against the pier.

"Excuse me," he said to the woman. She was in her mid-forties and her hair was in a single heavy braid. In the glow from the sodium light her cheeks looked greenish. He felt suddenly very weary, and he knew it showed in his voice. "My friend here has died and I am very tired. Could you let Harv know, up at the store? Please?"

He knew how tired and drained he must look, even without the weird effects of these new lights. She made an abortive surge in his direction, her mouth coming open; then she turned and trotted toward the shop, her weight booming the dock, her sneakers hissing. There was a sloshing sound as she hit the floating walkway.

Dick shipped his other oar and leaned forward, forearms across his knees again. He knew they were going to toss a raft of crud his way when they realized how many hours Dick had been gone.

Well, to hell with them. They hadn't been in the bays and around the south point and along the island and at the log. They didn't know.

And what the hell else could they do to him, anyway?

There was commotion and flurry and the cheesy bang of an aluminum door up at the shop. A lot of feet followed a lot of voices down the path and onto the dock. Dick let his shoulders drop and his head loll forward.

"Dick," he said quietly. "I love you bastards."

The man in the stern didn't say anything.

COUNTLESS STREAMS

BY DON ROBERTS

WITHIN THE LANE, A CANOPY OF GREEN TRANSLUCENCE transformed the light and air. The sunlight, bright and glaring on the highway, windshields flashing like silver salmon, became softer, tangible.

"It's a tunnel." Amy leaned toward Janet from the Datsun's back seat. At last the girl was unplugged from the Walkman worn every mile of the long drive up from Oakland. "An elf tunnel."

Davie scanned the scenery. "A bear, back in the trees!"

Amy's glance turned him to stone. Eight pushing sixteen, Janet thought.

"Maybe it's a Bigfoot!"

Amy touched Janet's shoulder. "An elf tunnel."

If elves are wild, unconcerned with humans. Janet breathed in and imagined she inhaled particles of light. "It is enchanted, isn't it? It's beautiful."

Dennis glanced at his wife.

It is, she thought. Full of death and pain, yet beautiful.

"Here?" Dennis slowed the car. "I can't get over how green it is."

Greenery blurred details. Horsetails massed in ditches, spreading up the right shoulder. Grasses grew waist-high.

Janet looked for landmarks. "Past those two mailboxes."

"I'd better make sure the drive's clear enough to get through." Dennis pulled over, stopped before entering the long drive. He turned off the engine and got out.

The children crowded forward. "Can I go?"

"Okay. Janet?"

"I'll wait."

"Be right back."

In seconds they vanished into the forest, voices reaching Janet with the locationless quality of birdcalls echoing around her. It was difficult to believe she was really on this road after all these years.

She remembered Tony, arm around her, waiting for the underground in London. They were on their honeymoon and sure they would be eternally together. "Seeds growing a brand-new age," said Tony. She remembered San Francisco, she and Tony lying together in their first shared bed as though their bodies had always known each other, the fog-horns calling one another through blanketed night.

She'd sworn she'd never return here, like she'd sworn never to sell the property. It existed in a state of limbo — Tony unable to convince Janet either to use or sell it. She could not live here and be reminded daily of her first son's death, yet to sell the property felt as if she were abandoning Bryan. He was still here, even if his body was buried in a Seattle cemetery.

Finally Dennis had spoken out. "Tony's right — let go, and let's move on from the past."

She wavered. Perhaps the time *was* right. She got out and stood beside the familiar red car.

"You okay?" Dennis appeared, crunching down the drive. He claimed to understand her need to visit one time to say farewell to the place; still, he thought it would be best if she had let him check out the property while she stayed in Seattle with Cindy, her friend who now drove a Skylark instead of a VW microbus and wouldn't think of grinding her own flour anymore.

"Where are the kids?" She couldn't hear them.

"Wanted to walk up to the cabin. We'll get there first — pass them on the way. Looks clear. Somebody's been out recently — Tony or realtors. Davie wants to 'scout' the drive for us."

"Dennis...."

"Don't worry, Honey. They'll be okay." He opened the door for her.

She hesitated. Don't worry, Honey? He had never seen how it can change — how quickly the joy of life vanishes.

"Janet. Let's do what we came for and go back to be with our friends."

She got in. Dennis headed the car up the drive before asking, "It's painful to return, isn't it?"

"Yes. More than I could have realized. It's as though Bryan is here."
Dennis nodded.

The kids were circling a stump. The car pulled in beside the shed.

"Can we take this toad home, Dad?"

Janet's reactions shifted swiftly. She couldn't focus on one feeling and give vent to it. She knew to Dennis she seemed withdrawn. She wasn't cut off from them or anything around her — on the contrary. Everything — children, cabin, the garden overgrown with nettles, the snag that Bryan called Camelot — overwhelmed her with rich sensations.

She ascended the steps Tony had built. Insects buzzed in the porch shadows. Inside, the cabin was bare, unfurnished (windows unwashed for how many years?), curtains gray and corners and rafters festooned with spiders and cobwebs. She climbed the dusty ladder to the loft and stood listening to the long-ago serenade of coyotes around the cabin. She'd wanted life to ring with novelties and surprises.

She returned downstairs, entered the alcove where she had tucked Bryan into bed night after night. Outside the window, she saw Tony on a day like today, beard red in the sunlight, carrying Bryan on his shoulders. Heard Tony's voice. He joked with his son, half singing: "Someday you will be a star."

She remembered monthly drives to Seattle, taking Bryan to the zoo or Science Center, visiting Pike Place Market, hanging out in cheap cafés.

She heard the creek, high with rainwater.

Before the alcove she wept, clutching herself to hold on to something threatening to slip away and be forever lost. Dennis entered the cabin and approached, reaching out to her. She shook her head and gently pushed him away. He handed her a handkerchief and left.

When she finally emerged, Dennis had the cooler out. He was handing sandwiches and apples to the kids.

"Something to eat?" he asked as she approached. "Leave those alone, Davie, they're dessert."

"No, thanks. Later."

"Why can't I have a brownie?" Davie asked her.

"Some juice? It's warm here."

She shook her head. "I'll look around. Visit a place of mine."

Davie grabbed the slice of apple Dennis extended. She watched Davie cram it into his mouth. Amy was leaning on her elbows, examining a butterfly resting on the thimbled spike of a lavender foxglove.

"I think we've got at least one flower child in the making here," Dennis said. "They must inherit it from you."

Janet said, "I'll walk along the creek." She moved away.

"Was Mommy crying?" Amy asked. Dennis replied in tones which became ever fainter as Janet left the clearing. Then Davie's voice cut through like a birdcall: "He's beautiful — why can't I take him?"

She saw Tony holding Bryan the first time, watching waving fists. "Bryan . . ." he said finally, "Golly!" That became his pet name for their son: Bryan Golly.

That morning almost four years later: Tony scolding Bryan for eating hot dogs when he spent a day with a friend. Bryan, angry and defiant, stomped off to be by himself. She questioned the scolding, the seriousness of the offense.

"We don't eat meat in this family," Tony insisted. "He knows that. Especially hot dogs. You know what junk's found in those things. Wouldn't eat them if I were a meat-eater. Said as much yourself."

"I know, Tony, but he's not even four years old!"

Jamming one hand into a pocket of his jeans, the pocket with a salmon stitched by Janet, Tony stomped off, much like Bryan, for Benson's, almost a mile down the road. He would trade refencing for goat's milk, and talk to Benson about setting a beehive in the clearing.

Bryan had taken the path to the creek. She waited a short while, then went down the path to talk to him.

The path was overgrown. She managed with detours to work her way down to the creek. Now and then children's voices rang out clearly through the trees. The forest was different than on that day: path now untended, vegetation of summer rather than early fall, the creek now full instead of trickling through a series of small pools.

Creekside vine maples glowed autumn crimson. Bryan, beside the small footbridge, looked back up the trail at her. She clasped one hand to her breast in histrionic manner. "What's this I see? Some enchantment of the forest or be it some young price, a bonny figure of a lad?"

He wasn't there. Hadn't been. Some trick of light fooled her into thinking she had seen Bryan waiting. Much later she would understand.

A crow flapped over her as she reached the bridge. That crow had given the black of its plumage to the days and nights of her life; its darkness became her own.

The pool beneath the bridge was lined with brown alder leaves. the water was not even fourteen inches deep. It was enough. She found Bryan face down in the water, the tea-brown water — his body still (*oh give me your noise, Bryan, your noisy liveliness*). Frantic, she felt for life. She tried desperately to breathe it back into him. As she struggled to the point of her exhaustion, she knew the figure by the footbridge had told her it was too late.

"Bryan?" she whispered.

No answer. He did not appear where he had that day. There was only the forest.

Janet waited where her firstborn had died, where he miraculously appeared. The forest pressed in upon her. Nothing left to see and nothing to wish good-bye. The creek was like countless streams that flow throughout the West. The bridge had fallen, planks covered with moss, fungus growing from the supports. The forest was as it was when she first saw it and as it would be long after she left it forever. She waited for Bryan to appear and make this parting.

If she knew where to look, just how to turn, that time and this time could come together as they were in her mind.

Davie's voice prodded her. "Indians! Wearing warpaint!"

She left. There was another place important to her. She would visit it and they could return to Seattle (where she had gone soon after the drowning, telling Tony she needed her good friend Cindy, the comforting only another woman could give, though she left ten days later for San Francisco because, she told Tony, she needed fog).

The path was steep enough to make a great sled run, if the snow ever fell deep enough to cover the undergrowth of sturdy deer fern, salal, and Oregon grape. At one point a fir, more than triple the diameter of her body, lay chest-high across her way. She had to reach to pull herself onto the log, and when she tried, she only succeeded in scraping the palms of her hands and her forearms.

Life and death intertwined around her. Decay and life spores were present side by side.

She sought passage underneath. Vegetation grew to within an inch or so of the bark. She might have been able to squeeze through if she were no bigger than Davie. She sighed and started searching for a way around the log.

She persevered, skin scraped and scratched in a dozen places. Familiar sounds floated up the slope to her. Hot and sweaty, Janet paused to catch her breath. Voices, her family, exploring the forest. She stepped between trunks of young hemlock and was there. Her special place.

The hemlocks formed a ring which had grown larger. The ground within the circle of trees was carpeted with needles, very little vegetation. A trillium was in bloom. Here and there a solitary frond of fern accented a rock or the sculpture of a fallen branch.

After a late-summer or fall rain there would be handfuls of delicate mushrooms or, early in spring, yellow violets here, there. The light within the ring always made her feel she'd stepped into a watercolor.

She sat upon a stone, touched the dainty ornaments on the red huckleberry growing from the stump beside her. Overhead, wind brushed through treetops, a sound she'd often ridden away on while in this place.

She was not alone within the ring. Fine hairs at the base of her neck stirred. She lifted her gaze above the carpet of needles. It might not be Bryan but some spirit dangerous to look upon.

Davie appeared, muddy to the knees, bits of bark and fern clinging to his hair and clothes. One cheek was scratched, bleeding a little, and there was a rip in the right knee of his pants. The pocket of his shirt was moving with the struggle of something within. He reached inside and pulled out a small toad. He set it on the ground between them.

Davie's toad was still a moment, then began hopping away. She rose and stumbled forward. "Davie, you're a sight." She brushed the bits of fern and moss and needles from his hair as wind moaned through the trees above their heads.

MADONNA

BY DAVID ALMON DOWNING

I

OWEN GANN LAY ON HIS BACK, EYES OPEN WIDE TO A VAULT of perfect darkness.

He needed to know what time it was. There hadn't been a clock in the bedroom since his family had left him nearly five years before. He had a watch, but never wore it — it blinked the time to the constant night of his sock drawer.

Through the frail walls of the mobile home he heard his daughter twist and push against sleep and sigh like a child. The fact of her presence brought him fully awake, and he worked his numbed face with the heels of his hands. Last night he'd listened to her get into bed, heard the light snick off and the surprised complaining of the bedsprings as she settled in. Now, straining, he heard her breathing, and paired his breath to hers.

After a time he swung his feet over the side of the bed and shuffled to the kitchen to start the coffee. Then he moved to the bathroom and stopped in the doorway, staring at the handle on the tank. Flushing it would wake her. He teetered there, scratching himself, until at last he turned away to the front door. Cool air washed over his bare skin. The wooden front step had perspired in the night and wet his feet as he padded down onto the cold, damp grass and moved around behind the trailer.

When he'd finished and started back, the sharp June night had begun to bite at him. Watching himself stride across the front window, his briefs glowing white before the darkened living room, it occurred to him that he needn't have worried about waking her: he remembered now to what violent depths Kim sank in sleep, recalled the contortions he'd found her in as a little girl, as if she'd fallen to her death from the sky. She'd sleep for hours yet.

He dressed and settled into his chair in the front room with his coffee and cigarette to wait for the day to begin. Outside, the cows were beginning to stir, their neckchains tinkling as they rose stiffly from the dry lot beyond the milking barn. The sky through the front window was now a tangible thing, lowering into place, a pregnant blue bleeding through the black. He'd spent his life watching the sky rise and fall over these buildings. So had his father and grandfather — a reflection Owen didn't pursue, because the line back suggested one ahead, and for years now that line hadn't existed. Owen was alone on the dairy, and that was how he felt it should be. His life had turned on a black night over twenty years before, when he'd stumbled over his stricken father in the mud of the cornfield. Since his boot caught the old man's head, pitching Owen to his hands and knees in the mud, his life had been a consistently declining and dwindling thing. He'd long since gotten used to it.

The sharp squealing of mattress springs jolted him, and the now lukewarm coffee lapped onto his wrist. Beneath his bare feet the floor trembled, and he could hear her footsteps. Owen held his breath and listened, letting the coffee drip from his wrist to the carpet.

Her door opened. More footfalls, and then a shaft of light fell into the hall from the bathroom for just an instant before she swung the door closed. The childlike sound of her at the toilet flustered him, and he ground out his cigarette and made much out of digging out and lighting another.

She would, of course, go back to bed. If she stayed, he'd find her propped in front of the TV when he came in for lunch. It seemed unlikely he'd ever know why she'd come back to the farm — not enough time would elapse before she left again for it to drift out of her. Last night he'd come in from milking to find her fixed before the glowing tube. How she got there he'd never know. There'd been no greeting; just, "I need to stay here. Mom said no." Unable to hold her flat gaze, he'd just nodded, head lost in exaggerated motion, and passed the hour before bed watching with her a story about rich people killing each other.

The bathroom door opened and light again fell into the hall and as quickly vanished. Her footsteps dissolved for him into a confusion of padded sound and vibration. When they ceased, he assumed she'd returned to bed.

Her appearance in the doorway, then, backlit by the kitchen's harsh light, took him a moment to absorb. When he did admit her presence to his mind it came all at once, like turning on a TV, an apparition that forced a small, dumb, surprised sound from him. Her hard white hair pulsed with light, and her eyes were black slits cut into her swollen face. She held herself, rocking slightly, in the doorway in her underwear and a ragged t-shirt, her short, sturdy legs glowing white. In her hand was a coffee cup, grey whorls of steam lifting from it against the blaring kitchen light.

"Cigarette." The word ground through her throat to him.

As she moved to him, hand outstretched, he swatted at his shirt pocket and around the chair before he found the pack behind his cup on the coffee table and shook half its contents onto the tabletop. He lifted one to her just as she reached him, then fastened his attention on replacing the cigarettes in the pack with thick, unsteady fingers.

"Light?"

He dropped the cigarette he'd just picked up and began patting himself for his lighter, each of his pockets in turn, between his legs and under him in the chair, along the sides of the cushion, the weight of her narrow eyes on him. At last she made a snorting, coughing sound, snatched his cigarette from him and pressed the tips together. In the orange glow until she got it lit, she looked old, older than she could possibly be.

Nineteen. She would be nineteen.

She kept the lighter and moved across from him to the couch.

With the cigarette back in the pack, he didn't know where to look, so he stayed hunched over the coffee table with his hands cradling his cup, monitoring her through his eyebrows. Her underwear was light blue, the t-shirt a tired white with the number twelve in blue tape on the front, and her legs were unnerving replicas of his wife's, squared and pale. Beneath the coffee table he knew her feet mirrored her mother's, too: blocked and tipped with toes like stunted mushrooms. She kept her elbows on her knees, cigarette and lighter in one hand, coffee cup in the other, her awful shock of brittle-looking hair alternately matted to and leaping from her head. *What do you want?* — his head talking to itself, his lips no more capable of moving the words outside than of speaking another language.

Gravel rolled in his stomach. He was thinking of his son Connie's visit year before last — his son transformed, completely replaced by a sour-toothed dying perversion of himself, skinned in black leather and spitting into an empty beer bottle. Like Kim, he'd just appeared, narrow eyes like knife-cuts. Connie had laughed at him, shook his head and mocked him to the friends that followed him (the mutant equivalent of friends, whom Owen couldn't help but stare at in their freakish costumes; as if an alien race had come to eat his food, drink their beer, pull their tiny, dirty alien girls into the back bedroom to smoke their dope). In only three days, Owen too had been transformed, into a bellowing, swollen image of himself, pushing and punching his son and his fat, stinking friend — both of them laughing at him, slapping at him like girls — out the door and across the yard. Back inside, he'd watched, panting like a dog, as Connie methodically shattered beer bottles in the driveway, maybe thirty of them from the back seat of his friend's corpse of a car, and then they left.

The last time he'd seen his son was a couple of days after that. Connie had returned silently in the middle of the night. Owen hadn't said anything when he found him unconscious on the couch in the morning, nor did he say anything when, that afternoon, the Yamhill County Sheriff had appeared to pick him up. While the Sheriff — a fat, easygoing man named Earl Easterday, whom Owen had known since grade school and always liked — guided him into the back seat, all three of them froze when the voice of Connie's mother came over the police radio, directing another car to another disaster. Clarice had only been a dispatcher then for a couple of months, promoted from the receptionist's job she'd taken when she'd moved into town with the kids. Earl, Owen and Connie had all stood stock still while her voice echoed off the mobile home and around the barnyard, moving like a ghost over the packed earth and gravel she'd crossed thousands of times. None of them looked at each other while they listened. When the voice cut out with an electronic cough, Earl finished putting Connie in the car and then did look at Owen, said he was sorry. Owen believed him, and appreciated it in a numb, detached way, but couldn't say anything or even nod to let him know. It didn't really matter.

After that, he fought off even thinking of Connie except as a child: a baby, a blonde toddler playing with a dog, patting a calf. Owen had learned to seal his mind from all but the distant past — and only selected moments from that, like snapshots in an album.

"How long till you have to go out?"

"Huh?" He'd heard her, but needed time to decode her torn sounds, to reconstruct the individual syllables into words, words into a sentence, and then formulate a response. As she repeated the question, he followed along, nodding, and was ready with his answer: "Not for a while."

"OK," she said, rose and went into the kitchen.

His coffee was cold, but he waited until she called him in for breakfast to refill it.

She took his cup from him, dumped the contents into the sink and poured him a fresh one. On the tiny dining room table were two plates filled with scrambled eggs of an artificial brightness; a plate of toast sat between them.

They ate in silence. The eggs had a rubbery, unhealthy taste. Owen wondered how long they'd been in the refrigerator. But he ate them all and thanked her when he finished.

"You're welcome," she said, standing unsteadily. "Just leave things. I'll clean up." She disappeared down the hall to the bathroom. Water ran, stopped, the toilet seat was set against the tank and in a moment he heard her retching. He looked at her eggs, then at his own.

He didn't know what to do.

It was time to get the cows in. He rose and went to his bedroom for socks, pausing briefly at the bathroom door, but she was quiet now.

Owen was milking the last group of cows when he glimpsed her hair bobbing through the calf barn out the milkhouse window. He moved to the door and pressed his forehead to the cool glass, watching her. She was doing chores, feeding the calves.

He'd waited for the eggs to turn on him, but nothing had happened. The rolling in his stomach now had nothing to do with breakfast, he knew. It was a gnawing tension of change, the uneasiness of seeing a stranger passing among his barns.

A screaming behind him rapped his head against the glass — one of the cows had kicked off her milker and it lay beneath her shrieking air into itself on the wet concrete. Hurrying to shut it up, he caught one of the panicked animal's hooves on his shin before he could drive his shoulder into her side and get to the machine.

Quiet restored but for the steady rhythm of the air compressor, he stayed leaning into her, his cheek pressed to her smooth, fragrant flank, and tried to quiet himself.

II

On the Fourth of July, almost a month after Kim's return, Owen sat on the front step waiting for darkness to come, waiting for the fireworks to light the sky over the fairgrounds. Watching them alone the last few years, staring out over the concrete foundation of what had once been the old farmhouse, had been a long, hard pull on him. The fairgrounds themselves were hidden from view across the valley by the cemetery's hill, on which tombstones were planted like crops. The foundation seemed of a piece with them: it was his family's grave marker, set for him in front of the individual plots — his grandparents', father's, his youngest daughter's — distant on that hill. Watching the fireworks beyond their dry, stony memorials had been the only other time of the year except Christmas — which he would never have back — that the pain became a live thing. It seemed to be connected to the electric sputterings of the fireworks, the sky's glittering explosions duplicated inside him.

But this year, there was Kim. He didn't know what would happen.

She was battering pots and pans in the kitchen after dinner, which she'd barbecued on the new, tiny grill sitting at Owen's feet. It had been delicious, the flavor of the steaks unlike anything he'd had before. Exasperated by his compliments, she'd snapped, "Dad. It's just a BARBECUE," and he'd stopped talking. He'd never had a barbecue, that he could recall, and the idea that he should warmed him.

Afraid she might miss the start of the show, he gathered himself to call for her, but heard her coming before he had to speak. The screen door rattled open and she sat down heavily next to him in baggy shorts and a big, shapeless shirt.

"Cigarette?" he said, holding the pack out to her.

She slapped it away and glared at him. "Look," she said, "I'm trying to quit, remember?" He apologized and looked back across the valley. He never knew when she'd take it and when she'd snap at him. She settled slowly next to him, set a glass bowl of cut carrots between her legs . . . and then snatched the cigarette from his fingers. Her drag on it was weak, clipped short, and she quickly passed it back to him. A tiny curl of smoke drifted from her nose but she abruptly retrieved it and passed a long, greedy moment with it trapped inside her before she finally sighed it away. "Carrots," she said, poking disgustedly in the bowl. "Carrots."

Owen flung the cigarette in a long, spark-showering arc to the driveway, then considered his daughter from the corners of his eyes. When the last of the cigarette's smell faded, it seemed to him that her body itself breathed — her cool, scrubbed scent washed over him. Fresh from the shower, how could she be cool in this close, breathless night? She must've taken a cold shower to fight the heat.

She asked quietly for a sip of his beer, and then together they looked out over the foundation, now fading to jagged silhouette against the pasture beyond it.

In a tired voice, she said, "How come you don't knock that thing down?"
"What?"

Her finger jabbed toward the low concrete wall and crumbled chimney. "THAT thing, that damn foundation. Knock it down, get it out of here so it doesn't stare you in the face. It makes me sick every time I see it."

A single rocket lifted up above the cemetery and squirted blue sparks into the sky. Its soft pop floated to them a moment after. The fireworks kept coming then, one at a time, the smoke from their explosions lit like quiet flowers in the twilight. Owen felt calm, almost sleepy, watching them.

He'd begun to clean the foundation up, but Clarice had shrieked at him to leave it alone. It had smoldered for days after the fire. The firemen tried to pick through it on Christmas day, but it was two days before it cooled enough for them to decide the fire had been started by a box of decorations set against a wall heater. On Christmas, the firemen gathered where Kim and Penny's room had been and filled a black plastic bag — Owen watched them fill it, zip it up and carry it away out of sight before its contents registered in him and dropped him to his knees. No one saw him fall. He'd seen a flash of light as they zipped the bag, the last glimpse he was to have of his youngest daughter, who'd crouched in her bedroom closet to escape the flames. A surviving shock of white-blonde hair.

It was her hair that had kept her from him, that had killed her; her hair, and her father's stupidity. It the chaos of clearing the house, Owen had run out on the lawn with Connie screaming in his arms to find his wife standing, mouth and eyes slack, with the girls below her on the grass. His family safe: Owen saw Kim and Penny sitting on the lawn with Kim's blanket draped over them. Penny's face was hidden from the flames, her hair drawing the fire's light. Kim watched the house fall with wide eyes. The firemen had come and moved hoses through the neighbors who had gathered to throw useless buckets of water on the blaze. Owen watched plump Rose Tether, their closest neighbor, kneel by the girls and heard her say to Kim, "Are you warm enough, Honey? Down here on the ground?" Though the house was giving off great blasts of heat, Kim lifted her arms to her and Rose Tether rose with her cradled to her cushioned breast. The blanket fell away from Penny, but she wasn't there. It *wasn't* Penny, but Kim's new doll, the big blonde-haired dolly they'd let her open on Christmas Eve.

Owen couldn't let his eyes return to the fire. He watched Rose Tether squat down for the blanket and tuck it around Kim. Kim whimpered, and Rose said, "You want your dolly, Hon?" and reached down for it, too, leaving a bare circle of pressed grass at her feet.

The sky over the fairgrounds had been dark for a while. Muted cracklings and poppings drifted across the valley; an occasional skyrocket rose meekly into the warm night air.

Owen watched Kim out of the corners of his eyes. Her ears were bare tonight, but he could see the four holes in the one closest to him. Usually she kept them loaded with tight gold and silver hoops, except the bottom hole, from which she hung all sorts of bizarre objects: heavy silver man-in-the-moon faces, tiny plastic wedges of cheese, delicate little gold cows, accurate to the nearly invisible teats on their udders. Catching him staring, she'd say, "Well, welcome to the monkey house. What are you gawking at?" or she'd tilt her head so they dangled free, clinking together: "Kind of like a mobile, huh? *FASCINATING* stuff."

She kept a straight face, but there was something nice about the bite in her voice.

She changed, in some way, every day. Her image constantly shifted, leaving him nothing to call up of her in his mind but invalidated pictures from the past. She'd asked him for five dollars a few days before, took the truck to town and came back with her hair sheared to within an inch of her head — and what was left, she dyed a pure, silky white. This had startled and confused him, seeing it for the first time. Everything seemed to remind him of something else since Kim had come back. He'd been plagued, sleeping and awake, by jagged bits of his past that he'd managed to subdue before her return. Every loss he'd suffered and had frozen from his mind had come back: his angry little brother walked through his sleep; the Christmas fire burned and crackled; his son grinned crookedly among broken glass, a skull on his shoulders where his head should've been; and the corn, dark and wet, scratched and rattled in the field. He'd awakened to the horror of coming on his dead father years before. They'd gone out looking for him, and after Owen tripped over him he had to pull the old man out of the freshly-irrigated muck. Now the sound of yanking him out returned to him as he changed pipe in the quickly-growing corn. Pulling his boots free of the mud, his heart raced.

And his daughter with her bristling, glowing hair had become the wavering image of all the children lost to him: his little brother, his lost baby daughter, Connie, Kim herself. When she'd asked him what he thought of it, he only mumbled something about her looking like a boy. She'd laughed at him, said he didn't know anything: now her hair was just like Madonna's. Owen didn't know who that was.

Now, in the sweet light of this evening, he was stunned by her. Still wet from her shower, her hair lay flat against her scalp and glowed a soft, snowy white over her tanned face. Her cheeks gleamed. For his daughter to have become this lovely (that word — "lovely" — came to him as if spoken aloud, looking at her), this lovely thing that she had now become — this left him lost in an alien emotion, his breath squeezed from him.

Her eyes flicked to him. "What are you staring at? I'm not even wearing any damn earrings." He turned back to the view and drew on his beer. "What?" she persisted. "What were you looking at?"

Expecting her expression to be difficult, her eyes to hold their past accusatory, faithless glint, he turned to find her smiling at him. "Come on," she said, and her white teeth snapped through a carrot stick.

He mumbled.

"What?"

The valley was quiet again. Looking back at the mountains, black against the luminous sky, he said, "You have a nice head. A really pretty head."

She sputtered at her carrot stick and her laughter's round, liquid notes bounced among the farm buildings. Shaking her head, she chose another carrot stick and said, grinning, "Well, thanks."

III

The foundation was tougher to bring down than he'd figured it would be. After he'd crumbled the blocks that had been baked by the fire's heat, what remained were stubborn, solid slabs of rock that barely cracked under his sledge. He'd thought about pounding at it with the tractor's hydraulic loader, but found he enjoyed the work. It became a constitutional, two hours in the sun with hammer and rock.

Soon after starting in on the foundation one afternoon, he drove a fat splinter into the meat between his thumb and forefinger — the sledge handle had split. He'd have to go to town for another one. His thick fingers were useless for the splinter, so he headed for the house to get a needle to dig it out.

Music was thumping through the front wall. Kim flashed by the living room window behind the vacuum cleaner, the machine's racket entirely consumed by the blaring music. She danced more than vac-uumed, pushing and pulling the machine with one hand, then the other, half the time going over already-vacuumed carpet. All very serious, almost grim business, judging by her expression.

The door was propped open, and he stood on the threshold waiting for her to notice him. He didn't want to frighten her. He leaned up against the doorjamb and crossed his arms over his chest, turning his face away, trying to keep his grin under control. Then he caught the heavy, sweet smell in the room, and his head snapped back around to her.

She caught the abrupt movement in her periphery and jumped, startled and goggle-eyed, scratching for the vacuum cleaner's power switch. She had to look down to find it. When the machine stopped, the absence of its whine was barely noticeable. She looked at the stereo, then at him, and then their eyes traveled together to the ashtray on the gleaming kitchen counter. A cigarette lay balanced on its lip, a narrow plume of smoke twisting up from it.

Without looking back to him, she stepped around the kitchen counter and ground the cigarette out. It fell apart, untwisted, its contents spilling into the tray. Still without meeting his gaze, she carried the ashtray past him, down the hall and into the bathroom. The toilet flushed. He waited for her to come out, but she didn't. He stared at the bathroom doorway.

Owen hated music, or tried to. Whenever he happened on the catch and moan of Merle Haggard or someone who sounded like him, he'd listen, but there was too much thumpy Hollywood-sounding stuff even on the country stations, halfway to that hard, weird, screaming music that had taken his little brother away from home years and years ago and kept him, finally, made him grow his hair long and get dirty and tattooed and lost. And now his son had been taken by similar music, but even meaner and louder, snarling music like spit flying; it had shaved Connie's head so his scalp gleamed like bone under his stubble.

The toilet flushed again, but still Kim didn't come out of the bathroom. The dope still hung heavy in the air, even though a breeze whipped through the room. Owen wondered if it was just in his head that he smelled it, just in his memory. His little brother Don had smoked it, too, though never near the house, or even close to the barns. Owen had caught him smoking it a few times, once with a pretty, shaggy-haired stranger of a girl he'd picked up at a concert in Eugene. Her feet were black as asphalt, Owen remembered, and when the two of them had looked up at him from where they sat leaning against the weedy fencerow, she'd started to pull her t-shirt down over her small, white, naked breasts, but stopped. She'd grinned sleepily at him as that smell hit him, and Don had collapsed, laughing, the laughter an affliction that seemed likely to kill him. The girl had just grinned from laughing Don to Owen and back again, her hands still on the hem of her t-shirt as if they didn't know whether to pull it down or lift it off over her head. Owen had left without a word before she decided. In just a few weeks, his little brother had his final blowup with their father and disappeared. He hadn't seen or heard from him once in the past . . . almost twenty years. Seventeen years. Their father died the year after Don left; Owen and Clarice's Penny would die the year after that.

Owen was lost. He looked around the living room, clean and scrubbed and bare of furniture but for the heap of it against one wall, and tried to think of just one thing, to hold onto a single thought without it floating to the next and to the next. He hadn't had this problem before Kim had returned. He'd had to remind himself to move to the next thought then; he'd settled into the cycle of the same ones, day in and day out, like a horse tied to a mill, plodding a ditch into the dirt. Now he never knew what he'd think, where he'd turn.

Kim stepped out of the bathroom, and as she approached, she kept her eyes on his. He couldn't figure out what was in them. She kept going past him, crossing to the stereo and turning the volume down. Owen had forgotten it was on. The quiet left him off-balance, blinking like a bright light had been snapped on.

"I'm sorry, Dad." Kim stood facing him, watching him intently. Then she leaned up against the far wall, pushed her hands into her pockets and stared at the carpet. "I don't do it all the time. I really don't. And I shouldn't, I won't. It's just that it's been a while, and it's . . . it's so good for housework." She glanced at him with a tiny smile, wincing, shrugging. The music whispered under her words, thumping like a heartbeat, then began to fade away. "It was the very last of my stash. It's gone. I . . . I know I shouldn't be doing it. It's dumb, it's dangerous, now. I'm sorry."

The first notes of a new song sighed from the stereo. Kim moaned, rolled her eyes, smiling. "God, I love this song." Keeping her eyes on him, she bent down and turned the volume up, but not too loud. This song was soothing, the woman's voice throaty and torn. "THIS is Madonna, Dad."

He nodded.

Laughing, she said, "Jesus, you're funny. And it's not just the dope, either. You crack me up all the time. You're, you're . . . you're CUTE. I never noticed. That face. You must've killed the girls. They must've wanted to take you home and dress you up or something. I'll bet. Like a big, shabby doll."

She pushed off the wall and started across toward him. His impulse was to step back, step back outside and down the steps, but he stayed where he was. There was something he should be saying to her — he should be angry, he should threaten to throw her out — but he couldn't speak. There weren't any words worth using. He just wanted to watch her, listen to her. The woman's voice in the song was hers, the same deep and strong pull to him, a sadness he wanted to wrap around himself like a blanket.

She kept coming until she was only inches away, smiling all the way, then stopped and looked at him like she was waiting for him to say something stupid so she'd have some reason to let go of the laugh he knew was waiting there. But he didn't say anything. Didn't breathe, even. She put her hands to his chest and shoved him gently against the doorjamb. "What?" she said, her teeth flashing. Face shining. "What goes ON in there, Pop? Hmm?"

She grabbed fistfuls of his shirt, pulled him away from the wall and then pushed him easily back against it. He kept his hands at his sides. "Do you ever relax? Would you just" — another shake — "loosen UP? What do you THINK about? You're like, you're like that . . . that Sphinx, you're like the Sphinx in Egypt. Mr. Stoneface. Mr. Rockhead. Old Rocky." She put her small, rough palm to his cheek and pushed his face gently to the side. When he looked back at her, the tiniest bit of a smile took over the corners of his mouth and she laughed and leaned against him, the top of her head fitting beneath his chin. She slipped her arms beneath his and elbowed them around her, and he was holding her.

"Dance with me, Rocky," she said. "No! No, no: Dusty. That's what Granddad used to call you, isn't it? Old Andrew." At once his eyes were fat with tears. They didn't fall, just sat there, burning. "I remember him calling you that. Sort of," she said. "Or maybe it was Mom who told me, one of the few times you came up." A soft, deep laugh pressed through her ribcage against his palms. Her skin cool through her t-shirt, miraculously cool despite the day's heat.

They were dancing, after a fashion. She had him rocking there on the carpet, turning slowly toward the middle of the room, pressed tight to him, his tiny, rock-solid daughter. That tightness in his chest that she gave him was a steel rod now, then relaxed, melted, then tightened again and fell away again, like he'd discovered a new muscle next to his heart — no, not new. Long dormant. He remembered feeling that way with Clarice, early on. Even later, after Kim. Even when she was pregnant with Penny. He remembered her calling him into the main house— their house, then, his father still living with his mother in this very mobile home while their son and heir raised his family in the big house. Clarice called Owen into the bedroom, and there she'd been, naked atop the covers at midday, her hands to her belly. It looked no different then, still her flat, smooth stomach, rippled with the marks Kim had left behind. He'd stood in the doorway, glanced over his shoulder, though he knew Kim was over with Andrew and his mother, that they were alone.

"It's another little girl, what do you want to bet?" Clarice had said when he turned back around, and the muscle in his chest had done this very same thing — flexing, resting, flexing, resting — and he'd gone to her and they'd made love all the afternoon, until they heard Kim calling for them and they'd looked around at the sheets and blankets they'd kicked off the bed in a heap and his clothes spread all over the floor and dresser, and they'd laughed — he remembered distinctly — and that extra muscle had tightened and relaxed . . .

The song was almost over before he became aware of his daughter again, the fact of his daughter in his arms, the hardness of her belly against him. The solid, pretty daughter of her solid, pretty mother...and the urgent hardness of her belly against him. The new, round hardness of her belly.

The single, salient fact of his daughter and his life now and his life to come was just suddenly there. He felt no surprise. Later, he'd wonder if he'd known already, if he'd known from that first morning's sickness and just hadn't acknowledged the thought. But all he did now was close his eyes and dance with her — and with the new, growing fact of their lives between them — dreading the end of the heartbroken song.

HELL IS A TOASTER OVEN

BY KATIE BRADY

NO DOUBT THERE WAS SOMETHING IN THE WORLD WORTH getting excited about, but Kelly didn't know what that might be.

Somewhere between the thunder of garbage trucks emptying dumpsters in the early morning and the demented yowling of cats in heat in the middle of the night, it (whatever *it* might be) was escaping her.

She had begun to get paranoid about this as she grew older. Suppose, at birth, everyone else in the world had been assigned a purpose in life, a destiny or vocation. And suppose the letter which would have led her to her own destiny had been misdirected, gotten lost in the mail, or delivered to another baby?

At this very moment in the jungles of New Guinea, maybe there was a confused young tribesman watching the sunset, scratching his head and wondering why he felt so weirdly compelled to build condominiums, wait tables, open a used car dealership, or write pornographic books . . . and unable to figure out why this compulsion seemed so strange and ill-fitting, like wearing someone else's shoes.

These thoughts plagued Kelly constantly, running in infinite babbling circles in her subconscious.

The garbage trucks arrived late one morning. Accustomed to being awakened by screeching industrial crash and rumble, Kelly became extremely annoyed when the ringing alarm clock woke her up first. Sitting up in bed, she reached over to the nightstand, grabbing the alarm clock and ripping its cord from the wall. Smoggy breeze blew in through the bedroom window as she sat there, staring at the offending clock in her hand.

A second later she pitched it out the window and reached for a smoke. As she lit the cigarette, there was a sound of glass and plastic breaking in the alley five stories below. Kelly took a long, slow drag, leaned back and smiled. It was a promising start to the day.

She left the apartment an hour later, climbing down the fire escape on the side to avoid running into the landlord. In the alley, she carefully stepped around the scattered and bleached bones of various appliances, dishes and ashtrays that had also soared out her window in the past few weeks. Kelly stopped for a moment, admiring her handiwork . . . the food processor and Waring blender had died beautifully, landing in a shower of broken parts and small, mangled motors.

When Kelly had been five years old, her parents had taken her to visit a wealthy aunt and uncle. While the adults drank and laughed in the living room, Kelly grew bored and began exploring the house. In one room was a small gymnasium, complete with a motorized exercise bicycle. Thinking it was a real bicycle with training wheels, she started to play with it and climbed up on the seat.

The motor somehow turned on. Kelly probably hit the switch by accident. The adults came running when she started to scream, and found her lying on the floor next to the running bicycle, her foot wrapped in the chain. Her uncle, a doctor, somberly examined her injured foot. He informed her parents that if Kelly had not been fortunate enough to be wearing thick-soled saddle shoes which jammed the meshing gears, her foot would have surely been amputated.

Kelly heard her parents relate this story over the years, but didn't recall it happening. Her mother used it to explain her daughter's compulsion to destroy appliances. Privately, though, Kelly was certain that it was prenatal imprinting, probably stemming from an incident when her mother had been frightened by a clothes dryer that caught fire.

Kelly suddenly frowned. A piece of broken white plastic reminded her of the coffeemaker she'd been given for Christmas. Kelly hated all appliances, but despised kitchen appliances most of all.

The day after Christmas, the new coffeemaker had sat on her kitchen table. Circling around the room, she warily examined it from every angle, even getting down on the floor to see how it looked from below. The very name "Mr. Coffee" offended her deeply. Did they think that by giving a courtesy title to an appliance she wouldn't have the heart to hurt it?

She had decided long ago that Mr. Coffee would plunge to his death. As she stepped out onto the street that morning, she made a mental note to place Mr. Coffee on the nightstand before retiring, in preparation for a dawn execution. She imagined, with no small amount of sadistic pleasure, that somewhere far away there was a Mrs. Coffee who would weep at the news of her sudden and unexpected widowhood, four tiny cups of fresh cappuccino clutching at her skirts in bewilderment.

Kelly caught the bus at the corner and closed her eyes, thinking about the day ahead at work. She loathed her job, and thought she might finally quit today.

For three months now — longer than she'd ever held a job before — she had sold storm windows by telephone in a tiny, claustrophobic room with four other mostly unemployable people like herself. The supervisor, Trask, was an evil slug of a man in droopy suspenders who shouted at her all day long.

From the first day, Trask had accused her of not taking the job seriously and not fulfilling her quota. Kelly had patiently explained to the red-faced goon that she could sell plenty of storm windows, if it weren't for the fact that her telephone was always out of order. Was it her fault Trask bought such cheap equipment?

Time and again, Trask had repaired her telephone only to have it out of order a day later. He'd even replaced it twice. As she left work yesterday, she had seen the repairman speaking to Trask, very quietly. The repairman must have discovered at last how she had been sabotaging the phone all along. Kelly knew it was time to quit.

The bus lurched into downtown, and Kelly dozed with her head against the window. She had a faint smile on her face as she dreamed of white refrigerators falling like lead bullets from the sky, followed by a thunderous cascade of washing machines that bounced off the pavement, high, high into the air.

Downtown was ugly, loud and filthy. Exhaust fumes. Industrial noise. Sparks from welding torches providing free fireworks. Mud-splattered cars. Schizophrenics standing on street corners, yelling at invisible tormenters who stuck hot needles in their eyes. Blank-eyed prostitutes and vomiting drunks clutching empty Thunderbird bottles. Snotty kids on skateboards commandeering the sidewalk, while prissy, overdressed legal secretaries leapt out of their way like a dozen Bambis fleeing a forest fire.

The ugliest part was the skyline, a mass of huge, mismatched, incredibly grotesque buildings representing some insecure real estate developer's phallic fantasies. The storm window company was in a crammed, windowless office high in one of these skyscrapers.

Kelly got off the bus and picked up a pack of cigarettes at a convenience store, strolling slowly in the direction of the office, stopping at intervals to admire rainbows glinting in oil slicks. The sun was still behind the clouds, but the oil managed to pick up a faint glow in the sky. This was always the last truly beautiful thing she saw in the morning.

Arriving at work was the most depressing part of the day.

From the moment Kelly breathed the first gust of artificially conditioned air that swooshed out the foyer door, she experienced a sharp pain somewhere in the depths of her soul. It was a familiar pain, one which she recognized as the instinctive discomfort experienced by a round peg being forced into a square hole. Since this wasn't her purpose or fated vocation — although she still didn't have a clue what really was— it meant a moment of brief suffering while her metabolism adjusted to the environment.

She had to take an express elevator to reach the office on the twenty-fifth floor. This only intensified the pain which was now burning a hole in her intestines. She couldn't stand the first few minutes when the elevator shot upwards and no floor numbers showed on the display. It was incredibly disconcerting to have the damn thing suddenly light up twenty, twenty-one, twenty-two, twenty-three. When the doors opened, she practically threw herself in the hallway . . . and after a few moments, the pains began to subside.

Trask was waiting for her at the doorway. Kelly had managed a smile and a falsely cheery "Good morning . . . " when he cut her off with a terse, "Save the bullshit, Kelly, you're fired. Go clean out your desk."

Having halfway expected this to happen, she wasn't upset — just a little disappointed that she hadn't gotten a chance to scream "I QUIT!" at the top of her lungs and march out with great drama and theatrics.

Kelly ruefully realized she should've quit last night, and not given him the pleasure of firing her. She knew she'd been caught again . . . why hadn't she just resigned?

She puzzled over this while filling a small cardboard cake box with her few personal possessions — a mug and a couple of chewed-up paperbacks she read during lunch. There didn't seem to be any logical answer, so she simply resolved never to make the same mistake again.

At the door, Kelly stopped and turned around as if she had forgotten something. Trask glowered at her, his face beet red, spittle forming at the corner of his mouth.

"Mr. Trask," she said as politely as possible, "you're a real asshole."

She was pleased to see that he looked as if he was about to explode as the door slammed shut behind her. She imagined the newspapers the next day carrying photos of the office, walls and ceilings sprayed with ugly pink flesh and suspender shrapnel. The headline would read: "Asshole Explodes. Story on Page Three."

As she waited for the elevator, Kelly planned the rest of her day. It was still early . . . she toyed with the idea of buying a couple of cheap electric can openers at Goodwill, just for the fun of it. Can openers were little solid, heavy things that made a satisfying THWACK on the pavement.

Remembering that she was now out of a job again, she decided instead just to go home and torture Mr. Coffee. She could hang him over the window ledge by his cord, so that he could see the broken and decaying corpses in the alley he would soon be joining. That'd kill the morning.

The express elevator softly chimed as its doors slid open again with an oily, snakelike hiss. Kelly got on, lost in thought as she once again pondered the Eternal Question of her unknown purpose in life, and punched the lobby button.

It was only a split-second, a fractionary stopwatch moment, before she felt her feet leaving the floor and experienced a weird kind of weightlessness. She was just beginning to enjoy the novel sensation, marvelling at how close her head was coming to the ceiling, when the malfunctioning elevator hit the concrete basement floor at one hundred seventy-five miles per hour.

The next day, the newspapers carried a horrifying photograph of mangled, twisted steel and cables laying in a heap at the bottom of a deep, dark elevator shaft. The headlines read: "Local Woman Killed in Freak Mishap. Story on Page Three."

WHITE HORSE MEADOWS

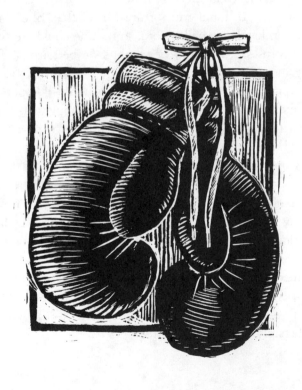

BY MARJORIE ROMMEL

WHITE HORSE MEADOWS — August 17, 1986 —
Police here report the late-night arrest of an elderly drunk
who, refused entrance into his son's new home, filled a child's
yellow sand bucket with new-planted lawn and flung it
through the front window, breaking a ten-dollar pane.

A SMALL WIND BLEW INTO WHITE HORSE MEADOWS. IT SET long-legged blue marguerites dancing among stiff-necked geraniums in the window boxes out front of the Model Home Office.

It turned up the silver undersides of grass blades growing almost tall enough to mow along the new sidewalk, skittered among beauty bark not yet turned gray around marching throngs of marigolds, and circled the sign that read in pleasant homey script — geranium red on white — "Come Right In!"

A quiet wind, but not without some strength, it was the kind of breeze that, to a person who knew anything at all about the weather, signified change.

Harvey Sussman, his dark green polyester tie loosened and the first button of his short-sleeved green shirt undone, stood outside the office, enjoying the breeze. He sighted along the sidewalk side of Appaloosa Lane, where several young families already had begun to make themselves very much at home.

If he squinted his eye just right, he could screen out the lumpish gray piles of dirt and rubble and raw-looking foundation forms on the lane's other side, could see — as if in a vision — what White Horse Meadows would be, in just a few months' time.

At the third house from the end of what Sussman thought of as the "good" side of Appaloosa Lane, he could see Martin Hoodenpyle on an aluminum stepladder putting a third coat of white paint on the trim of his new, yellow Victorian-style farmhouse, which had twelve-paned windows in front, and an old-fashioned veranda around two sides.

Sussman chuckled to himself, thinking how Hoodenpyle, his pretty, chubby wife Marion and their two bored kids had made pests of themselves poring over the plans for their new house, haunting the building site, demanding unscheduled changes at every turn, finally moving in before the paint was dry; how each morning, now they were in, Hoodenpyle was out prowling the perimeter of his newly-acquired turf, kicking fenceposts as if each was a suspect tire, checking each stake and side of string around his new lawn, which was just now sprouting like a bald man's hope for hair.

Proprietary, he decided. That was the word for Martin Hoodenpyle.

Sussman grinned, hitched his white belt around his bulging real estate salesman's waistline, and turned back into the hot office, toward his bed and the television in the back, his refrigerator full of beer.

The sun, yellow-orange as a marigold floating among white beauty bark clouds, prepared to sink over the western rim of Martin Hoodenpyle's tidy world, and as it did so, the wind picked up. Harv Sussman, thinking of Vanna White and Mr. Weinhardt's Private Reserve, closed his door.

Martin Hoodenpyle, humming on his ladder, sent a wave after the older man once he was sure it would not be seen.

Sussman, he knew, would talk and talk, going on about the legendary deals he had made, the developments he had filled, what a gold mine White Horse Meadows would be for him, the buyers, the builder, everyone. Meanwhile, the smells of supper cooking would be growing stronger by the minute, and when Marion came to the door to call him in — "Oh! Mr. Sussman!" she would say. "Won't you stay for dinner, too?"

But Hoodenpyle did not want Sussman in his house at his table eating his food with his mouth open, his napkin shoved between two shirt buttons, awkwardly displacing his bilious tie, the children goggle-eyed as he forked roll after fresh-baked roll from the basket set not quite far enough out of his prodigious reach.

But now, Sussman was safely inside the Model Home Office, a beer in one hand and dulcet Vanna White turning her white throat and arms in front of him; Hoodenpyle knew he was safe.

He afforded himself a moment's pure thrill in the ownership of this seventy-five by one hundred ten foot piece of land: the trim yellow and white house he had caused to be built upon it, the flat and springing new green lawn he had planted around it, his son's red BMX bike with all the chrome trimmings neatly kick-standed in the drive, his daughter's pink Smurfette Big Wheel parked next to it, the pink, blue and white streamers on its handlebars lifting and rustling in the wind, which lifted to him the smell of salmon grilling on the patio, the clean smell of white paint rising from the bucket only just under his nose.

Hoodenpyle sighed his satisfaction, pushed up his glasses, and once more picked up his brush. He dipped it, making a fine point of the bristles loaded with thick white paint, and applied it lovingly over the second coat, which he'd put on only the day before.

Dinner was, of course, wonderful: the grilled salmon steaks, fettucini with fresh basil and cream, chilled asparagus à la vinaigrette followed by a splendid peach sorbet. Marion was, Martin considered, as superb a cook as she was mother and housekeeper. He beamed at her plump, aproned form bustling in and out of the kitchen.

The children, already bathed and fed, watched the Bill Cosby Show in their Superman and Smurfette pajamas while their parents dined. The polished teak table was set with linen, fresh flowers, good china, and wine goblets filled with a rosé as sparkling as the prismed Austrian crystal chandelier.

Rosy sunset light coming through the twelve-paned bay windows touched a flame to the couple's matching blond heads so that nine-year-old Michael, coming into the room for another roll during commercials, laughed.

"You look just like that picture of Grandpa Dutch," he giggled, pointing at Martin's temporarily fiery head.

Outside, a dust devil formed on one of the Morgan Lane construction sites two streets over whirled cross-lots to fling gray grit at the Hoodenpyles' front windows and onto the Hoodenpyles' new front lawn.

An hour later, the dust had settled, inside as well as out, and Michael, released from "Bench Time" in his red and blue Superman motif bedroom, joined four-year-old Melody in her Smurfy pink and white nest for a bedtime read. Melody's choice was *The Three Billy Goats Gruff*, which never failed to scare her silly, giving her an excuse to stay up at least another half hour, and thereby getting one up on Michael, who had the bigger bike.

"Not fair," Michael grumbled.

But by ten p.m. the house was quiet, the blonde kiddies snoring gently in their beds, the dishes cleared away into the dishwasher. The happy householders, Marion and Martin, in their matching blue and white terry robes and scuffs, were cozily watching the evening news.

"Mind explaining what all that was about?" Marion inquired drily, her pink-nailed hands wrapped around a cold glass of seltzer and orange juice.

Martin grunted, his usual answer to questions centering on his father.

Marion finished her seltzer, watching her truculent husband from under thick yellow lashes, retrieved the newspapers littering the floor around his chair, and went quietly to bed.

It was a long time before Martin joined her.

Out on the main highway several miles distant, an old man stumbled along the moonlit shoulder, thumb held at arm's length and down, as if to condemn to the junkyard all passing cars for their drivers' refusal to abandon set destinations in favor of his, which was far less clear.

A green Ford convertible with the top down roared past, full of screaming girls, their waving arms and hair whipping like so many flags. Next, a Mack truck, whose driver hauled a short blast on his air horn in salute or warning — the old man was not sure which — then a Greyhound bus deadheading for the barn, followed by nothing for a very long while.

The old man staggered out into the middle of the highway, stood on the white line waving his overcoat, his brown-paper-sack-swaddled bottle.

"I have a son, damn you all, you can't do this to me," he shouted down the empty road.

He took off his hat, revealing skimps of hair that might once have been red, searched with dirty fingers inside the hatband for a slip of paper he seemed to remember putting there for safekeeping some while ago. Just how long ago he could not recall.

Absorbed with the hatband, the old man was startled into a scream by the rapid advancement of what looked like the twin headlights of a very big car with no intention of slowing down for anything, least of all for him. He clapped the hat on his head, both hands over it, ducked and began to run.

The car revealed itself to be a pair of huge, shiny motorcycles, their headlamps separating as the cycles roared around the ancient drunk in the road, their drivers' blatting laughter carried back over their shoulders to him as they continued down the road.

"Damn you, I have a son," he yelled again, more to himself than to any part, wheeled or otherwise, of a world that seemed to be moving far too fast for him, and in the wrong direction.

Three days later, it was supper time again in White Horse Meadows, the sun once more on the westward slope of Martin Hoodenpyle's roof on Appaloosa Lane, gliding down the ridgepole as it had done, these many summer nights, in a marigold blaze.

This time it was steak, the best New York cut, grilling on the patio which sent up its exotic steam.

The grass now was a soft green fur, and, the shutters pristine in their fourth coat of white paint, Hoodenpyle had moved his folding aluminum ladder to the back yard, where he was at work fixing a bird house, a yellow and white replica of his own, to the top of a meticulously white-painted pole.

Melody splashed happily in a Smurf-colored wading pool closely watched by her fond parents, one on the ladder, one at the grill. "Look at me," she squealed. "Watch this." She jumped up and down in the shallow water, causing the ruffles on her blue Smurfsuit to bounce.

At this moment, Michael, who had been skidding up and down the gravel lane on his red BMX bike practicing Evel Knievel–style leaps over chunks of firewood, his sister's pink Smurfmobile and the cat, caught the whiff of steak grilling and turned back toward home.

He hauled to a stop outside the Model Home Office, arrested by the sight of a strange man stooped outside his house, trying to see inside.

An old guy in broken shoes, baggy pants hung from knotted suspenders slung over a plaid flannel shirt, black overcoat over one arm, brown hat flopped on his head like an unworthy thought, like something a flying cow might have deposited there.

Michael, drop-jawed at the vision of this particular old man who, he noted instantly, had the remains of what might once have been red hair sticking out from under that awful hat, suddenly became aware of his heart thudding under his tank top. Looking down, he could see its movement under the orange cloth.

The boy startled painfully when the real estate salesman touched him on the arm. "Says he's your grandpa," Sussman offered in his froggy voice, nodding down the hill.

Together, Michael and Sussman stood surveying the scene, both with intense interest, Michael's tinged with a dark feeling in his stomach he was still too young to recognize as foreboding.

Below them, the old man bobbed and wove like the prizefighter he once had been — slower, of course, and less sure on his feet — as he worked his way along the sidewalk first in one direction, then the other, angling for the best view inside, or around back of his son's house, where he figured all the action was.

Finding the perfect vantage point, Michael's own secret watching place at the north corner of the lot behind a clump of vine maples left to redden decoratively on a small hummock near the road, the old man began inching forward, nudging, as he did so, the string that cordoned off Michael's father's new lawn.

In the back yard, on his ladder, Martin Hoodenpyle turned quickly around, testing the air for wind.

At this moment, there was none. But like a rangy spider hurrying to check any small vibration to its web, Hoodenpyle rappeled down the rungs, tense and ready to deal with . . . what? His too-rambunctious son crashing his BMX into the newly-laid lawn?

Fists clenched and sandy hair bristling, Hoodenpyle made the northeast corner of his new home on two wheels, Sussman thought, watching, feeling Michael tense with fear next to him, and came face to face with his own unexpected father peering at him through screens of alcohol and vine maple with glad and needy eyes.

"Marty?" his father ventured.

"Oh Jesus. Oh shit," Michael heard his father reply.

From his post near lumpy Sussman, himself a kind of comforting hill, Michael watched his father stop, advance, turn around at the very edge of that much-protected patch of grass, tramping down a small circle, then retreat toward the back yard.

"Marion," Michael heard his father bawl.

Dutch Hoodenpyle's only grandson heard his father yell for his mother, not so much his usual order but a plea for help even a ten-year-old could recognize, though Michael was not yet ten years old.

Michael saw his mother come out on the front porch, still armed with the barbecue mitt and fork, saw her hover tentatively near the rail waiting to hear what was needed, heard his father bark, and his mother, closely flanked by soggy, shivering Melody, turn back into the living room and abruptly close the door.

The dull thud of the door's closing, solid and heavy as half a heartbeat, came to him on the wind, which, through holding its breath, had again begun to rise.

It brought to him the smell of steak burning.

Michael watched the old man untangle himself from the vine maple and his father's string fence, watched him cross the lane, climb a pile of dirt and sit down on top.

At the top of his new roost, Dutch Hoodenpyle, never taking his eyes off the neat yellow and white house, pulled a paper-wrapped bottle out of an overcoat pocket and took a long, shaky drink.

Michael, remembering his father's response to his suggestion of resemblance to the old man on the rubble heap, was tempted to avoid further trouble by sneaking home the back way, unseen. But some kind of fellow feeling for the shambling duffer overcame him, and, bidding Sussman good night, he wheeled bravely down the lane and into the drive. He parked his bike neatly where his father had told him always to park, and marched up to the house as if he, too, were a visitor to his father's door.

It was locked.

Michael rang for his mother, and as he waited for her to open, he turned for another look at the old man across the street. The red plaid flannel arm, cuff turned back a jaunty turn and a half, waved, bottle in hand, a kind of paper-bagged salute.

Michael grinned. His own arm was lifted as the door opened. His father grabbed him by the orange shirtfront and dragged him inside.

It was a long, troubled evening inside the Hoodenpyle house on Appaloosa Lane.

The sunset, more a slice of dead daffodil than marigold, winked out under cover of lowering clouds. And the wind, such a merry, prankish breeze these last few days, gathered strength enough to topple Michael's red bike off its kickstand, bang the white shutters against the house, loosen leaves prematurely gold from the vine maple, plastering them against the sidewalk and front porch like a chorus of pleading hands.

Shifting quarters, the wind blew fistfuls of gray subsoil against the Hoodenpyles' west windows from the rubble heaps across the way, threw apart the rough plywood shelter the old man had built for himself.

Then the rain began: fat, warm drops spotting the dust, pooling into rivulets that formed tributaries and islands as it ran down into the coat-lined nest where the old man slept off his booze.

Later, it chilled to a downpour that leaked off his hat and into Michael's red, white and blue Superman bedroom, where a defect in the roof flashing, somehow undetected by his father, let in the rain.

More resourceful than ever he would have imagined, Michael tiptoed down the hall for one of the yellow plastic sand buckets he knew were on the back porch. He would set it under the leak, then take his sleeping bag to Melody's room where he would spend the night.

As he crossed the hallway, the boy heard above the drone of the TV news his mother's calm voice and his father's, wrathful and petulant.

Quietly, he slid open the patio door, padded out for the bucket, surprised by the strength of rain, and aware of his grandfather sitting on top of the trash heap across the street. Too far away for lamplight, still, he could see the outline of the old man's sodden hat and black overcoat, could see the miniature marigold fire of a cigarette, could smell its slightly acrid smoke.

"Hi, Grandpa," he whispered. He grabbed the bucket, slipped back into the house and closed the door.

Marion, in her own way as sensitive as her husband to minute changes in the uneasy atmosphere of their perfect home, felt her son abroad and went to check. Finding a puddle, she began pulling fresh pajamas from Michael's drawer, moving quietly so Martin would not hear — he was so angered by Michael's faults —and took the sheets off the bed.

When Michael returned, she was surprised to find his shoulders damp, but his pants were dry.

Together, they moved the bed, set the bucket, replaced the sheets. As she tucked him in again, he asked, "Mom, why does Dad hate Grandpa?"

Marion sighed. "I don't know that he does, Michael. Go to sleep now. Life will be good again in the morning."

She turned toward the door.

"Grandpa was a fighter, wasn't he?" Michael whispered after her. "Mr. Sussman says he was famous, a real barnstormer." His voice sounded eager and proud. Marion wondered if a former punch-drunk turned real drunk might not prove a better hero for a small boy than daredevil Evel Knievel, who, it seemed to her, was bent on a different, more contagious kind of self-destruction.

Perhaps even better, she thought disloyally, than a father so closed in on his own past, so closed off from the world that he could not abide burned steak, imperfectly washed dishes, birds snatching seed from his new lawn, his son's occasional youthful incontinence, his daughter's clumsiness, the suspicion that his wife might sometimes think differently than he . . . never mind the untidy arrival of a father he'd never forgiven for some grave fault he wouldn't, or couldn't, seem to name.

"Good night, Michael. I love you," she whispered, then closed the door.

In his bedroom at the back of the Model Home Office, Harvey Sussman found himself unable to fall asleep, thinking about Martin Hoodenpyle and his old man, Dancing Dutch Hoodenpyle.

All evening, he'd paced between the beer-stocked refrigerator, his reclining chair in front of the TV, his bed, and the window, where he kept looking out, knowing perfectly well it was too dark to see anything, but needing to look anyway.

It boggled the mind, thinking one was the son of the other, the father, the grandfather. What could have happened between the two of them, that they should greet each other so? Why wouldn't the son let his father in? And what the hell could that old man be doing, down there on that rubbish heap? What did he want, anyway?

Sussman's feet were cold. Catching a flash of light in the corner of one eye, he sat up one more time in the ruin of his twisted bed, heaved his feet over the side, and in the dark, planted one set of toes square in the tinfoil tray left over from his TV dinner. There was hot sauce left in it.

Kicking and cussing, Sussman wiped his foot on the rug, and, hitching up his pajama pants, sidled up to the uncurtained window. Sure enough, the porch light was on at Hoodenpyle's. Was somebody going to let that wet old man in after all?

That would be a relief; then he could sleep.

Sussman saw Michael come out on the porch and snag the yellow bucket, accidentally tipping the other one off the porch, where it rolled around in the yard. The boy went back inside. But before the door closed, did the kid wave? Harv ducked back, afraid he'd be seen. It was then he spied the old man's cigarette glowing in the dark like a single eye.

"Aw, Jesus and Mary," he said, and began pulling on his clothes.

Across the street from his son's new home, Dancing Dutch Hoodenpyle hunkered down among the rocks, wood and concrete ends of a construction site and, with Harv Sussman and a new case of Weinhardt's squatting beside him, fell to brooding over his life, his many triumphs in the ring.

Triumphs that others, he told Sussman, including most notably his own wife and only son, had seen as failures. He thought on the filial impiety of that son.

"Honor thy father. That's what the Good Book says."

"A man should be proud of his family," Sussman returned, thinking of his own war hero father, his long-dead wife and her wealthy brothers with their no-good sons. Sleeping Jesus, the things you didn't see in this business.

His own father, Dutch recalled, settling into the rush of the booze, had been an itinerant preacher and sometimes Watkins products salesman. Taking young Dutch with him, he made his rounds in a battered Chrysler up and down dirt country roads, stopping in at the primitive homes of housewives who had, at best, like his own mother, linoleum floors and running water; at worst, no electricity, no water, and cracks big enough that swept dirt never reached the door.

Out of Dutch's mouth into Sussman's sympathetic ears, the years peeled back easily until, toward the end of the second bottle the old fighter had hidden away in his coat pocket for a rainy day, he began once more to think how his son, then the age of that spindle-shanked boy on the red bike — what was his name, Michael? — had turned away from him a little more each time he returned home bearing gifts: an autographed glove, a signed bout poster, clippings in which sports columnists spoke of his legendary roundhouse swing, his near misses, his reputation outside the ring.

The boy's mother, he complained to Sussman, was a stiff, unforgiving woman. Somewhere along the path of years, she died, and the boy went to live with her old-maid aunt in a place it had taken him, Dutch, a long time to find.

What had the boy's life been like with that old woman? Sussman wondered.

"Books, that's what," Dutch snorted. "Lots of books. But never no sports, sure as hell no boxing or wrestling." That was Fern's wish, he explained, passed on thin-lipped and glaring to her Aunt Heather, he was sure.

"But the boy fooled 'em," Dutch hooted, tipping down another beer. "He took up numbers and computers instead of the lawyer's outfit that united female front served up at him with every hard cookie or plate of thin stew."

Grade school, high school, then college; Dutch told how the boy had climbed carefully, soberly up each rung, never once asking him, his own near-famous father, for advice or the favor of an autograph for his friends.

Sussman listened as Dancing Dutch talked, telling how gradually, over the years, the road home looped back less often as he saw his son turn from him first in what now seemed as if it might have been shame, then in anger, and finally with contempt.

The night wore on, the rain came down, and together on the rubbish heap the two old men got drunker and colder.

"Come on back to my place," Sussman said for perhaps the fiftieth time, as together they struggled to replace the plywood shelter, anchor and shore it up. "I got stuff to eat, and dry clothes. And you can have the bed."

But Dutch wouldn't budge.

"What the hell are you waiting for?" Sussman demanded, his patience frayed. "That kid of yours would have you arrested before he'd let you in."

Dutch stuck out his chin and stared over it, belligerently, fixing the real estate salesman with a haughty glare as he, without looking, opened his third pint, this one the Old Granddad he had given himself when he stumbled across Marty's grown-up path at last.

"I don't recall inviting you to share my shack here," he growled. "You want to go home, go home. No skin off my back."

Old Granddad. Those kids, that skinny boy and his sister, the little blonde dumpling with the high-pitched squeal, they might be calling him that right now, if Marty's wife hadn't shoved them inside like so many chickens, then closed the door.

He might even be sitting inside that house with them, he thought, eating a piece of the pie he'd seen his son's wife — what's her name, Mary? — take out of the oven, maybe even topped with a scoop of real ice cream sided with hot coffee and a tot of good brandy to warm him up, untie the knots. That boy, so much like Marty was, he'd love the stories his old Grandpa Dutch could tell.

But, Dutch reflected out loud, "I can't blame the woman. It appears she's a good mother to those children, a good wife to Marty, too."

In the time he'd been sitting there, watching his son's family, he told Sussman, she'd never been still, always moving about with that fine, firm way she had, picking things up, putting them down, clearing away, baking, cooking, washing up, speaking quietly to the kids.

"A good woman knows how to be useful," Sussman observed.

"If nothing else in the world is right, a person at least ought to be of some use," Dutch raised his voice and hands, moving into a harangue.

"People ought to take care of each other, help each other out when they need it."

Just like he had helped his buddy Jim "Socker" Wilson stay out of the hands of those guys from the hospital, he told Sussman. They'd wanted to pin Socker's hands up around him in a white jacket just because he'd busted up a bar that time in Portland.

A man can't be of use when he's locked up in a hospital, he'd told Jim then, feeling the righteousness course through his veins. Socker was just a little bit punch-drunk, that was all. He hadn't meant to hurt anyone.

His mind slid away from the fact that his friend had busted up several bars, not just one, the bartenders too, that he had eventually died in a fall from a hotel balcony.

"My head. There's something wrong with my head, Dutchy."

Dutch could still hear the Socker's words, still see the way his friend's face had twisted with the effort to figure it all out.

"You going to come home with me or not?" Sussman demanded. Soaked and chilled far beyond his small endurance, he wanted his warm room, his bed, the comforting society of his TV, which required no conversation or agreement, and which did not argue back.

"You want to go home? Go home!" Dutch Hoodenpyle roared at him.

Sussman went.

Some time later, the old man woke with a start. The wind had changed and the rain had stopped. A small light shone a welcoming, perhaps a forgiving gleam somewhere deep inside his son's cozy home.

Such a nightmare, he thought, accusing him of being the real thief of his son's childhood. Dreams of his son's eyes, now set in his grandson's face, turned sadly, wistfully, toward his father's retreating back. Dreams of his father's face — his own, so many years younger — turned gaily, eagerly, toward the road, the ring, freedom.

Freedom from what? Certainly not from bruises, broken bones — his own and others — cauliflower ears, a booze-soaked brain he was sure moved separately inside his skull each time he shook his head. Had the Socker's been like that?

And the road; it was one of those Möbius strips where you started out in one place and ended back there again, thinking all the time you were headed somewhere else.

When he was young, it had been wonderful, setting out to make his fortune, driving cars till they broke down, then catching a bus or a train or plane, hitching rides or walking from one ring to another, each scheduled bout a chance at fame.

Mornings, especially, were wonderful on the road. When you passed through a place in the daytime, all you saw were the people rushing back and forth like so many mindless ants. At night you saw nothing but the mystery of lighted railway stations, crossing lights, the blinking neon "Vacancy" signs in front of the fleabag motels.

But in the mornings, early, the world was new, if you were traveling. The houses and the buildings were there, all right, but somehow you didn't see them. It was the land itself which made itself felt in the first light of day, huge and permanent and somehow tolerant of all this human foolishness.

Once, on the way to a fight in California, when he still had a manager and a car and good clothes, a satin jacket, red with white lapels and his name, *Dancing Dutch Hoodenpyle*, embroidered on the back, he had stayed the night in a fancy Portland hotel. He'd closed the bar, then, back in his room, watched old TV movies, one starring Jimmy Cagney, his favorite.

Early next morning, while it was still dark, he'd heard a sort of tapping in the bathroom and had known it was Cagney, telling him in some kind of crazy Morse code to stop dancing, give up the road, go home.

But he just couldn't do it.

He'd closed himself in the bathroom for hours, practicing Cagney's steps, the ones he'd heard, loving the way the tiled walls and high ceiling sent back the sound, exhilarated nearly out of control by his own movement.

He'd gone on to California. It was his one big chance. So were they all.

How could he, true knight of the road, have given life to this stick-in-the-mud son?

But then, there was Socker. And after Socker, the road seemed to slant downhill, the Möbius strip unglued or twisted so he never got where he was going, never got back to where he was from, either, and finally ended up here on this rubbish heap, useful to no one, not even himself.

Water he was sure was not rain tapdanced down his face, and full of self-pity, Dancing Dutch Hoodenpyle bowed his head on his huddled knees.

Let the damned sky leak down the back of his neck. Let him die of pneumonia. They would, damn them all.

"My son," he said to himself, the words bitter in his mouth as the taste of dead leaves.

The rain drummed on his plywood roof (dead Cagney signaling him again) and after a while the old man lifted his head, looked again toward the marigold glow of the night light in his son's kitchen.

Those kids need a granddad, he told himself.

Then, showered with applause, Dancing Dutch Hoodenpyle rose from his corner, grandly shucked his red satin dressing gown, and, lumbering across the street through the strings surrounding his son's new lawn, waltzed into the ring.

SUMMERS BY TRAPP

BY JEANNE E. SCHULTZ

TRAPP BUMPED HIS CENTURION LEMANS BICYCLE UP THE gutter on the west side of the North Cascades Highway. With one turn on the pedal his spokes glittered toward the air/water box beside the gas pumps. Lights of the only all-night store between Sedro Wooley and Winthrop flashed on his helmet.

Trapp leaned his rear wheel against the metal box when a thin smile stretched his lips. Sector three, time Mark: 2140, nine-forty at night, with a full moon. Trapp slid the helmet off his sweated temples and threw back his head.

His plan all checked, except that Trapp stood alone.

A minute later he hacked and spit to clear the residue he carried outside from the clerk's Kool cigarette. The orange juice in plastic helped cool his mind.

"Nice shorts." He strode toward the men's room wondering if the bottle-bleached clerk had really said that, and to him. He wanted another look at her neck, where it joined her collarbone.

Trapp's fingers stretched. He calculated millimeters of change for flex to extension, but sights intruded. A tan VW bus slumped behind a cyclone fence, its rear wheel missing. The front tire was flat.

"Flat . . ." he thought. "An accident." A picture of his own black spandex shorts splattered on the pavement, flashed.

"Switch!" Trapp re-programmed. Above the gas pumps an advertising poster showed blue-black speeding wheels. He used the picture to cancel his fear.

With the past a hundred miles behind him in Seattle, memories of the wrong girl rested in a Neanderthal era buried under a thousand thought-years. She was ancient prehistory. Still, Trapp only breathed well with feet in the toe clips.

His hand slipped on the night sweat of the metal doorknob as he left the men's room. Calculating again, millimeters, relative humidity, he walked. With his eyes low he blocked the fence and the wrecked VW out of his life. A concrete seam led him to the air/water box and his bicycle.

Orange juice stalled in his throat, warm. Trapp wanted it cold to chill the trouble that crept from his stomach in dead times like these. When he was climbing, power-breathing, when he took aim on the pavement, he didn't have to think.

He stood staring back through the window of the convenience store when a blue flyzapper above the clerk's head cracked another victim. Trapp leaned over to pull out the water hose so he could aim it at his forehead.

"Gotcha," the clerk mouthed with an exhale. Her eyes trained on the stripes across Trapp's chest.

He stared back, then flapped his eyes shut against the icy water. He let the numbing black temperature take him until it turned inside out, emerging as orange heat.

Over the Rainy Pass summit, Trapp shifted into a higher gear. The fading signs for Early Winters Resort got only a whir from his gears as he slid through the dark. His headlight sent a quivering beam fifteen feet ahead: useless. He steered by moonlight, and manipulated geometric formulas to occupy his mind. Designs by Trapp, for airfoils, and a steam generator to run his headlight; these formed and bloomed in his brain through the foothills and into the dawn on the Methow Valley.

Trapp filed his mental patents and moved on to review the toll-free phone number he'd need to follow up on his tardy subscription to *Physics News* magazine, which he had ordered fifteen weeks previously. He planned to call from Winthrop, early. With the time zones he could ambush a witless circulation manager.

The sun rose over hillocks. Dusted ray settled on a low rise that dipped to some historic creek and rose again. The contour seemed familiar, like something he might care for if he let it rest on his mind.

Trapp shifted into a hill. He looked down on the hillocks. He was surprised to discover that he was distracted.

Reviewing his major goals he gave an extra snap on the pedal for each success: Ninth grade summer, bike to WSU, with Les. Les had been chummy, not at all serious. Les had wanted to leave Grand Coulee turbines long ahead of Trapp. They were near a fight until Trapp allowed a major concession of the schedule and sent Les ahead to make camp. Les never did because he found some bored girls in a Winnebago.

Grade ten, Continental Divide, top of the world; and the shale oil project of the Rockies, with Robert. That time Robert lingered. He delayed by hiking to a waterfall where he went on at length about the mining runoff and soil erosion. Robert had assumed they would ride together again but Trapp didn't want any spies from the Sierra Club around his neck.

Graduation, cum laude, destination: Chicago Museum of Diesel Mechanics, with a girl.

A rock chip shot, snapped on the rim of the Lemans. It shot up. Trapp winced but went on though blood mingled with the sweat across his shoe top.

With a girl. She had the brains, the money, the looks, but she quit before they even started. All she had to do was carry her gear and keep up. She quit.

Trapp reviewed their conversations, the hours of planning. He had considered every detail. He couldn't have been wrong about her.

The rising road made him push hard as he looked out across the hillocks again. With the sun up behind them, Trapp blinked. His mind scoped back six hours to the clerk with the sculptured neck. Her memory rose like the hillocks, like nature in art, and art in a body.

At Three-Fingered Jack's Tavern in Winthrop, exactly on schedule, Trapp stretched himself across the doorway to share the air-conditioning with his armpits. The phone on the far wall gleamed through smoky shadows. Trapp wondered if AM/PM numbers were listed and if this trip might be different.

THE IVORY GLASSES

BY KIMBERLY M. REASON

NO ONE KNEW, OR HAD THE NERVE TO ASK, THE NAME OF the old lady who lived in the gothic, spooky house. Without ceremony, then, she was clumsily referred to as "The Old Lady in the House." Later, when enough gumption was conjured to explore her outside residence, dark ropes hanging from the ceiling in her padlocked garage caused us to call her "the witch" and her garage, "the dungeon."

Jill, our older friend and babysitter, cruelly stirred our terror by concocting a fearsome tale of agony and death concerning the witch. "I've heard that those ropes were used to hang kids who'd sneak in her yard so she could torture them!" she told us as we played dodgeball against the squat, concrete wall kitty-corner from the garage. She prodded us with ridicule — "Don't be a scaredy-cat!" — to confirm her knowledge until we hoisted one another up far enough to peer through the small, grimy windows of the dungeon door. Within the blackness of its interior, we could make out chains or ropes or something, suspended and still. Reluctantly (because no one wanted to give Jill the satisfaction of acknowledgement) a kid halfheartedly agreed.

"Yeah, I see 'em."

"Does she kill people?" asked Thomas, forehead crunched into a question of concern as he nervously sucked on his thumb. He was a munchkin-sized boy of six who lived with his grandmother in a small, avocado-green house trimmed the rich brown of fudge. Jill, inflated with authority, had been waiting for such a leading question.

"Of *course*, dummy!" Her contempt was insincere, appearing only for show; she was glad for his ignorance. It presented an opportunity to elaborate on her lie. Thomas twitched indignantly at the insult.

"You don't have to — "

"Shhh!" cautioned Monica in a fierce whisper. "I think I hear the witch coming!" True enough, a feeble cry came from the sea-green depths of an overgrown back yard.

"You kids stop playin' 'round my property!" fought the wrinkled voice as it struggled through a maze of thick vines and gargantuan dandelion weeds coated with fine, white needles.

"Shut up, you ol' witch!" yelled Jill, hurling the statement less to subdue the old woman than to boost her image among the group.

"I'm no witch!" the old woman retorted, voice quivering in anger, or maybe sorrow. "Wish I was! I'd do something to you kids!" A distant crash of leaves punctuated her threat, sending us scrambling like cockroaches from the scene of guilt, screaming in glee and theatrical fear.

Curiosity getting the best of us, the next day we crawled along the ledge surrounding her house, daring to catch sight of the witch through her window. Beyond the dirt-caked glass were vaguely visible scant pieces of furniture: an overstuffed chair spewing stiff clouds of yellow cotton, a fast-food restaurant table with wads of dried gum affixed to its black leg, mismatched with a chrome chair that obviously belonged to an absentee kitchenette set. A stand-up, fireside-chat radio sat silent in a dusty corner, its torn speaker screen and missing knobs lamenting its uselessness. Large, faded roses woven into a dull pink, threadbare carpet were in spots hidden by stringy throw rugs. A ray of sun illuminating a square column of swirling dust particles pierced the otherwise lifeless scene.

Hardly satisfied, too innocent to appreciate the stark loneliness revealed by the view, we discussed proving our valor by creeping through her yard of carnivorous (said Jill) plants to get to the witch's back door. We were convinced terrible things were going on in the kitchen. "I swear, this morning I just saw somebody get chopped up with a big ol' butcher knife!" reported Jill, big-eyed. "And she hangs the pieces in her kitchen to dry!"

A sight too gruesome to pass up, we formed a three-person posse to accomplish our investigation. Monica, born leader of the group, would be first in line to head the expedition. Derik, a good fighter (he once beat up a boy three years older than himself) would guard against the preying swoops of flesh-loving plants and other enemies. And me, too, wanting desperately to prove, more to myself than anyone else, that I was not a sissy, because sissies lost out on all the fun; this would be my debut into a real-life adventure from those safely pursued in children's mystery books. Our goal: to confirm Jill's accounts and confiscate evidence to bring back to the police when we reported the witch's murderous rampages.

On D-day, a silent crowd of buddies, curiously without Jill, gathered into a respectful, coaching audience. "Bring back an ear," requested one in a hush. "Don't get caught!" advised Thomas, plucking his thumb into his mouth. We made a formidable team. Derik, small but mean, carried a rubber sword he'd received two years ago for Christmas. From afar it looked real: the blade, maybe two feet long, was painted a grey color fused with silver flecks so that, if held just so, the reflection of the sun on its surface shot a mystical light-beam of power. "Excalibur," he murmured to himself, swishing the weapon magnificently through the air before replacing it in the red plastic sheath along his side. Boys staying behind looked on, envious.

Monica arrived with a diminutive pair of binoculars sculpted from ivory and trimmed with polished brass draped daintily about her neck. Wings of dirty hands, anxious to try them, fluttered and grabbed, but she was quick to twirl away. "These are my mother's!" she warned everyone. "I had to sneak them out of the house, so don't touch 'em or they might get broken!" The sanctity of forbidden possessions subdued the group, causing everyone to change their approach to awed caution. After closer inspection, Jimmy was not impressed.

"Those don't look like the kind on TV!" he complained, mouth pulled into his usual sneer. To him, "real" binoculars were big and black, like the kind used in *The Wild Kingdom*. "Yeah," agreed another. "Why are they so small?"

"Because they're *opera* glasses, stupid!" replied Monica, rolling her eyes upward.

Monica lived in a house nicer than most on the block, though by outside standards it was closer to working- than middle-class, tacky for its deliberate ostentation. A Greco-style statue of a nude man spouting water through a raised torch stood incongruously on the small lawn; an overabundance of flowers and exotic shrubs, mismatched in color and size, betrayed amateur efforts at landscaping.

Her father, much to the chagrin of her mother's snooty relatives, had been moderately successful at selling commercial refrigerators, allowing his wife to make a show of maintaining her pseudo-bourgeois roots. Thus, among her schedule of cultured activities she attended the ballet and opera; the glasses decorating Monica's budding chest were a family heirloom.

"Couldn't you get some real ones?" Jimmy asked, disquieted now, for he was aware that the kids were sniggering at him, not that prissy know-it-all, Monica. He always resented her for being better off than anybody else, a perception proven to him by her long curls and starched dresses (insisted upon by her mother) and the natural way she assumed leadership of the group.

Without warning, an alien shout interrupted us. "You kids git from around here! I told you I don't want you playin' 'round my property!" Suddenly we were reminded of our mission. Monica, wildly flapping her arms behind her, beckoned everyone to run around to the blind side of the garage. Pairs of small legs and feet ran as if on rice-paper to hide, heels clattering musically across the pavement. Straining to hear, we waited.

"You kids hear me?" came a query. Silence. "I'll call the police!" she warned, almost hopeful. With effort she listened, peering through her dense foliage.

Jimmy caught sight of her from his vantage point near the ledge. Excited (no one had ever seen her from this close) he crouched down for an undetected eyeful.

And a wicked witch she was! Her aged face mimicked a forgotten Halloween pumpkin left too long in the window, caving into itself as it rots. Crevices of a cruel life pinched toward the center, emphasizing a puffy, twisted nose. Her mouth curled in an ugly fashion, as if she was hounded by a putrid, persistent odor. White hair — or what remained of it — stiffly jutted from beneath a scarf bound tightly under her chin. Small, dark eyes, narrow with suspicion, burrowed deeply into her forehead. Her ancient body was large, stuffed like Polish sausage into dark, tattered clothing.

A breeze came along and bit her with its chill; grumbling, she retreated inside. Hearing the click of the door we rustled to suppressed life, forming quick, breathless plans. With Monica leading the way and Derik bringing up the rear, we would first scout the back yard for clues left behind over the years. Then, we would climb her back porch and look through the kitchen window; or if the window was beyond reach, we'd open the door a crack for a look inside (this last made us shudder with the gravity of our commitment).

Jimmy, puffed up with the triumph of his exclusive sighting, recounted the event. Enraptured, we listened: he was a valuable asset to the group. The contagion of his self-importance added weight to the significance of our mission while sealing him in as a permanent member.

Finally we were ready to embark. Those not coming found bushes, fences, and cars to hide behind for surreptitious observation. We came to a second hush as Monica tiptoed in her patent-leather shoes to the iron-rung gate of the backyard. She used her binoculars to peer between the licorice-twisted bars, finding cobwebs and their inhabitants, one or two cigarette butts, a candy wrapper, but mostly grass and leaves. She shook her head at Derik and me, mouthing: "NOTH-ING." Derik poked me in the shoulder blades to move on. I glanced back, annoyed.

"Go *on,*" he pressed.

"I am!" I whispered harshly, throwing him a dirty look. With his chocolate skin, lush curls and light brown eyes, Derik was the cutest boy for blocks around. At one time or another all the girls in the neighborhood had had crushes on him. But he often irritated me; he played rough, preferring a stinging slap to get your attention, or throwing the ball extra hard to get you out in games. He released a loud sigh of exasperation. I continued forward.

As we approached Monica she raised the lever of the gate and eased it open, wincing to herself as the stiff, lazy hinges squeaked and groaned. We stopped, glancing apprehensively toward the porch, and wondering if the witch had heard. There was no indication she had. With that, we began our ascent.

The cement steps had begun to chafe in the center, disintegrating as if dying. The stairway, dark with the umbrella of overgrowth, snagged and delayed us in a network of sticky spider lines. At the same time, long blades of grass reached hungrily out to us, dancing across our skin. The bitter scent of weeds raced to confront newcomers, warning that we were penetrating unexplored territory. We paused at the top of the stairs, pretending to plan our next move but actually recollecting our scurrying nerve. Something dark edged over my shoulder: a giant snake unwrapping to snatch me away! My stomach twisted and flipped as I whirled around with a gasp.

"Derik!" I hissed, finding his sword. With effort I stood on knees weak with the rushing relief of fear's egress. "*Watch* it!" He went on to raise leafage with the tip of his sword, allowing him a glimpse into bug-buzzing interiors as each of us moved off to explore separate corners of the yard. The preponderance of brush was overwhelming; clearly, the yard had not been tended to in years. A rusty park bench, one side resting on a cinderblock, was propped off-balance under a cherry tree, white splats of bird waste mottling the bleached, wooden slabs of its seat. The surrounding ground was stained crimson by seasons of fallen cherries. Tired leaves crunched like potato chips beneath our strides.

"Look!" said Monica, swinging her head around to me. She had found a strangled vegetable garden and was on her hands and knees, intently peering at something. Both of us joined her on all fours and became riveted by what appeared to be the carcass of an animal. Leaning closer, we found it to be the shell of a dead cat. Derik poked at it with his weapon, dragging the cadaver out from hiding. Beige in color, it was a hard, empty form void of eyes, fat and entrails. Its mouth was stretched agape in a petrified yawn of agony, the legs fanned out in an eternal dash for escape. None of us had ever seen a dead animal — save for the crushed flatness of birds in streets — and were fascinated by the combined results of preservation and decomposition.

"She kills animals, too!" said Derik, struck by the meaningful discovery of our first piece of evidence. We glanced around to one another.

"How do you think she did it?" I asked, using curiosity to hide my rising fear. None of us had any ideas, except to revisit privately the one of being in the witch's yard; nobody wanted to end up like that cat. Monica straightened and began backing away, looking around as if expecting the hand of death to swoop from the sky.

Derik resumed his poking at the cat, still intrigued by the effects of long-set rigor mortis. A thought struck him: positioning his sword directly above the creature, he brought it down with determined force. The cracking sound of the impact coincided with a piercing scream from Monica. Our hearts raced to our throats. We sprang from our quarry, glancing in the direction of her cry. Anxiety gripped us: where *was* she? Another scream! Running to the edge of the yard, we came to what looked to be a deep ditch.

Several feet below lay Monica on her back, kicking frantically and unable to right herself on a yielding bed of blackberry bushes. Sharp thorns were tearing dotted, red lines into her bare-skinned legs. Prickly vines caught her hair and entangled themselves there, smothering and scratching her face. Their home disturbed, insects swirled madly about, some landing upon and biting into her blood-flecked body. She looked as if the earth and its creatures were swallowing her.

"Help me!" she pleaded, the first signs of panic showing themselves. All we could think of was somehow or other pulling her out; we lay on our bellies but it was clear before we even tried that our arms were too short to reach her. Imagining herself entrapped in the snare of the witch's sorcery, strangled by the carnivorous plants of which Jill spoke, Monica's frustrated sobs ballooned to loud, terror-flushed wails.

Noises of doubt and surprise, already surfacing from our audience in the alley since Monica's initial screams, rose to din of what-to-do. "Monica! She'll — "

The sound of a nearby, creaking door: the witch! Fear gripped the walls of our bellies and balled into tight fists. We began panicking too, whizzing our heads to and fro as if expecting help from a miracle. I suppressed an instinct to run, to leave Monica to what Fate or the witch had for her.

There came from the alley a chorus of cries and clamoring feet as our witnesses, realizing the ominous turn of events, disassociated themselves from the project. Fading shouts rebounded in the air. Their abandonment filled us with dread.

"*Quiet*, Monica!" admonished Derik under his breath, twisting a peek over his shoulder. "She'll hear you!" But in the throes of her horror Monica completely lost control. She began to hyperventilate, choking on her sobs. Ringlets once carefully styled now drooped in a pathetic bevy of hair noodles.

"What are we gonna do?" begged Derik, peering beseechingly at me.

"I told you kids — " the witch's voice stopped. From the porch she could see patches of clothing in the near distance. She peeled her eyes in disbelief; why, those nagging little devils were in her yard! Her annoyance switched to shrill anger, years of bitterness now given an external outlet. Grasping the iron banister with her left hand, she grabbed her cane with her right. Refusing to move quickly, her decrepit body painstakingly made its way down the steps.

"What *are* we gonna do?" repeated Derik. He was jumpy, out of place, a soldier good for action but not in formulating a course for one. My eyes darted through the terrain, searching madly for possibilities. Then it came to me.

"The vines!" I answered. Across the ditch stood a wire fence interwoven with beefy ropes of green growing down the opposite wall of the hole.

"I'm gonna show you kids!" shouted the old woman, sounding closer. "Trespassin'! You're trespassin' on my property!" The trembling fury in her voice shot electric fear through our bones. Monica, now whimpering helplessly, had not moved from her prostrate position.

"Monica! Grab the vines and pull yourself up!" My finger jabbed towards the fence, but all she could do was blubber stupidly at me. I stole a glimpse to my rear and caught first sight of the scary old woman. She was ugly and mean-looking, just like Jimmy had said. Her size was imposing: big, like a sturdy peasant who had spent her life plowing stubborn fields. "GRAB THE VINES, MONICA!" I was shouting now, trying to jar her to action. The witch raised her cane at us.

"You little heathens! I'm gonna tan your hides! You got no right!" She was moving towards us with progressing speed, her face red and puffing with angry intakes of breath, hands taking hold of whatever gave balance along the way. Frantically, I shot instructions to Derik and Monica.

"Derik! Lay down and pull her up with your sword! Monica! Grab hold of those vines and climb out! *Hurry!*" Monica finally managed to gain enough composure to move, crying out as thorns dug persistently into her. She began to weakly scale the root-strewn wall of the ditch, her feet slipping every few steps but nonetheless making gradual headway. She was halfway up when the proximity of the witch, now just a few feet away, prompted Derik to advance bravely on the old woman.

"Back off, you witch!" he commanded, pointing his sword at her. Fear had turned into purpose: Derik was now in his element. The boy's audacity sent shivers of rage through the woman. Raising her cane, she lunged at him. With the agility of youth lacking in his opponent, Derik dodged the attack. Unable to recover from this unusually quick movement, the old woman continued in the direction of her thrust, falling against a large, round bush. She grabbed a handful of leaves and twigs, tightly clutching them until the momentum of her fall slowed and stopped.

"I'm gonna knock you out, you old witch!" warned Derik. He was hopping in place like a boxer, stabbing his sword in her direction. Truthfully, he was only bluffing. Hitting an old woman was too alien a thought; a far-off dictum of Respect Your Elders was strong enough to cause him a little shame. Nonetheless, he hoped his threats would stop her.

But the woman was resilient and worked up. Pulling herself to free-standing, she swiped again at Derik, catching him on the jaw. The rubber shoe of the cane buffered the strike somewhat, but slammed his teeth against his tongue in an excruciating pinch. He doubled over in acute pain, groaning through the pool of blood filling his mouth. The woman raised the cane again, meaning to bring it down on his back.

"Look out, Derik!" I yelled just as Monica, now aground, held onto the wire fence to steady herself. Instinctively, he blindly sliced his sword upward through the air, cutting the arc of her swing. The cane was knocked from her hand and, flying like a poorly-launched javelin, punctured a dense mass of leaves, disappearing. By this time Monica and I had reached Derik. Running to him, I grabbed his blood-stained t-shirt and pulled him with us towards the gate.

As we ran past her, the old woman reached out and grabbed one of Monica's ringlets, giving a sharp tug. A long curl, like a lifeless garden snake, came off in her hand.

Monica screamed as her neck snapped back, but did not stop. Lost in blind terror, desperate to escape, we stumbled down the crumbling steps, rolling into one another as we poured into the deserted alley. Without hesitation or words we continued to run, run, until each of us was safely locked away in our homes.

Mrs. Isabel McAvery screeched upon the disheveled and bleeding sight of her daughter. "Monica . . . ?" she asked in disbelief, cupping her child's face into trembling hands. Her little girl was a mess. The once crisp, yellow dress was now torn and black with dirt, a frayed ruffled hem dangling to her knees. Monica's legs were full of small holes and deep scratches, half-hardened streams of blood streaking her shins and calves. The ringlet torn from Monica's head had been a small one; nonetheless, there was now a raw, bald spot where it had once been.

Mrs. McAvery's first horrible thought was that her daughter had been molested. She was reaching for the phone to call the police when it rang. It was Derik's mother, Anne.

"Anne, I can't talk now! I think Monica's been attacked! I've — "

"No, Isabel!" Anne interrupted, "It was the old lady down the block! It seems the kids were in her yard and   "

"Old *lady?*" Isabel couldn't imagine . . .

"Yeah, you know, the one who lives in that spooky house?" Anne went on to repeat Derik's account. With intense relief, Isabel drew Monica protectively close to her as she listened, incredulous. Afterwards she insisted that the police be called, but Anne talked her into meeting at the old woman's house to set a few things straight.

Mr. and Mrs. Davies were accustomed to their son's frequent brawls. Both considered Derik's fights routine — a normal boy's rite of passage. They were not alarmed, then, when Derik came home in a bloody shirt. "Whose butt did you kick now, boy?" asked Mr. Davies from his low point in the recliner. A dark, stocky man, Mr. Davies had also fought his way through growing up; for his stubby appearance he had been called Buddha by neighborhood kids. It had taken very un-Buddha-like tactics before they began using his christened name.

Out of breath, Derik told the harrowing tale. When he finished he was told that he'd gotten what he deserved; on the other hand, if anyone was going to impart corporal punishment on his son, it would be Mr. Davies, not some old lady in the neighborhood. Therefore, while Derik received belt lashings for trespassing in someone else's yard, his wife made arrangements with Isabel to confront the old woman.

But there was no confrontation — direct, anyway — to be had. The woman merely shouted through her locked door, the same thing she'd told the kids: "Git off my property! I'll call the police!"

After half an hour of door-banging and recriminations, Anne and Isabel left the porch and went to the latter's home. There, they reviewed the idea of calling the police; after all, the children *had* been assaulted!

A few cups of Irish coffee subdued their maternal ire. Instead they gossiped about similar events in their own lives, eventually agreeing that the kids had learned a good lesson. They doubted if the children would ever bother the old lady again.

They were right. We considered ourselves lucky to have narrowly escaped the witch's wrath, only part of which had been proven that day in her yard. And although we stayed clear of the house, the fearful encounter had left an indelible mark on our group dynamic.

Since our brush with her and successful escape, Derik and I had established a mutually respectful bond. I'd been the one who'd pulled us through that day; as a result, he now turned to me for leadership, and everyone else followed suit. Monica, embarrassed by her poor performance (and mercilessly reminded of it by Jimmy) lost her unquestioning hold over the group. In an unspoken way she became an outcast, playing with us less and less until she stopped altogether.

The re-telling of our hair-raising adventure soon wore too thin for further interest. We moved our gathering ground to a discovered treehouse up the hill. Summer passed into other adventures, and save for one or two glimpses of her, we all but forgot the old witch woman.

One hot, Indian summer day in September, an ambulance pulled into our street. Seeing the flashing lights from the uppermost branches of the tree, Jimmy made the announcement: "Hey! Somebody's at the witch's house!"

We scrambled down knobbed limbs toward the scene, our deadened interest in the woman momentarily revived. Noticing the activity from her bedroom window, Monica couldn't resist joining us as two men in white carried a burdened stretcher down the witch's front steps.

"What's that?" asked Thomas, pointing with his free hand. Whatever lay beneath the sheet was oddly shaped and peaking in various places, giving rise to a range of mini-mountains. We encircled the stretcher, squeezing in between the orderlies. Bored and seeing room for a morbid joke, one of the men threw back the sheet!

"Danny!" admonished the other. But the deed was done. In unison the group gasped and flowed back like a wave, retreating from the horrid sight and rush of sickening odor. Thomas gagged on his thumb and jerked it out of his mouth, gawking at what lay in front of him.

On the stretcher was the old witch, her mouth frozen open in a triumphant grimace as if stubbornly delivering to the world her last, defiant insult. The skin on her face sagged like a poorly-pitched tent over protruding bones and eyeless sockets; a filthy scarf hung loosely around her head, which was now truly sunken in from death's touch.

Derik and I regarded one another, an identical thought moving between us: she looked just like that dead cat. But what truly made us tremble were her arms, stretched upward. In her hands, tightly gripped, were the ivory glasses.

"The glasses!" breathed Monica, transfixed. We all stared in disbelief, plunging into the vertigo of vivid recall: the smells and textures of a fear once laid to rest enveloped us with relentless clarity. Monica lurched forward to take them, then stopped, frightened of the old woman, still.

"She's got a death grip on 'em, that's for sure!" laughed Danny, enjoying the sadistic thrill. "You can bet those babies gonna be buried with the old cow, right, Paul?" He snapped his head toward his partner, grinning.

Paul pursed his lips in disapproval, taking the free corners of the sheet and re-covering the hideous form. In an effort to take the sting out of the exhibition, he offered an explanation.

"We got a call from the folks next door. Seems they noticed a bad smell coming from somewhere in the back of the house. They searched it out, came across her lying in the ditch back there," he jerked a curled thumb in that direction. "Guess she fell in and couldn't get out."

"Kicked the bucket trying!" piped Danny.

Paul gave him a hard stare. "When we pulled her out," he said, "That's when we saw the binoculars."

There was a pause as everyone eyed the glasses. "Looks like," he concluded, "she went in there for 'em."

SAINT CALIXTUS' EAR

BY JAMES G. POWERS, S.J., Ph.D.

FEW MOVEMENTS ESCAPED THE VIGILANT EYE OF TAD RULLY, in his twelfth year as resident gravedigger at Saint Calixtus' Cemetery, a rock-skip from the Canadian border.

Tad was christened Theodore at the insistence of a devout mother. Like Sarah, she had borne barrenness until, as she saw it, "God gave" this son, whose precious arrival into the world was to be oddly associated with others' departure from it. To say that Tad excelled in his calling is not overstatement. The record revealed one who, other than abiding two weeks' yearly vacation, had missed only five work days in his long tenure. "He's a sturdy one," chuckled his uncle Emory. "That's from working close to the soil!" And with a well-creased snicker: "I don't think he'll ever give up the ghost!"

Tad, like an Exocet, targeted a white envelope which fluttered from the purse of the grieving figure, who, supported on the plump arm of Monsignor William J. Pouter, stumbled from the canopied gravesite towards her limousine. The Lincoln was parked two hundred feet away, dominating like a doberman an elbow of road bordered by three sullen yew trees. The caretaker scurried to the fallen paper, noticed the prestigious law firm's name, then deftly managed to thrust another sealed letter into the tearful woman's hand. She continued to dab her eyes, but, in her agitation, began using the envelope instead of the tissue originally extracted from her bag. The confusion portended an irony only time would ripen.

Monsignor Pouter, the solicitous escort who observed this muddle, was a porcine prelate, a native of Wisconsin, whose fervent devotion to its cheese had shaped him, finally, into a sphere not unlike a cheddar wheel. His loping walk had earned him the sobriquet "Barge" from his clerical associates. He repaid their attention by cultivating a rigid smile that one might read on the slit lips of a gout victim standing in an interminable smörgåsbord line. But that frozen crease was not his only trait; he also managed to cultivate a flock whose precarious state of soul was relieved somewhat by the stable state of their securities. Among these needed and needy clients, Ms. Astoria Flushing, the aggrieved, escorted lady, could certainly be numbered.

Born Elsie Madsen, sole child of a logger and companion who survived on the rugged north coast of Washington, she resolved young to leave the Evergreen State for lusher pastures. This Elsie successfully accomplished after her graduation from high school, with the assistance of a floater, a stubby marmot-like ally, seven years older than she. His affluent father gladly provided him the liberty to roam through life with few obligations, save occasionally intercepting a healthy subsidy to perpetuate his pilgrimage. Lester Ellison clumsily affected the image of a social apostate, committed only to himself. "I'm not killing myself for nobody!" he would solemnly announce, convinced of his delphic eminence in an otherwise miasmic world.

To be sure, Elsie resonated to Lester's sour altruism and religiously supported his creed of comfort through others. This tenet she quietly pledged never to renounce.

Lester and Elsie's relationship did not pulsate with passion; any titillation focused on travel. For five years the two confederates strolled along the trestle of distraction, which provided resourceful Elsie with an advanced degree in genteel living, as well as considerable expertise in emulating the insouciance of the rich: from the elegance of Hawaii's "Pink Palace," whose tanned and pampered denizens made lethargy respectable, to Rome's *Via Condotti*, where profusions of silk cascaded from every window, complemented by supple mounds of lambskin gloves and stylish brocaded purses. These conjured the logger's daughter to embrace a world of breeding and luxury, whatever the cost.

Then Lester's savage death brought all to an abrupt halt! Majorca's *Costa del Calma* ironically hosted the brutality: a victim trussed up like Saint Sebastian, patron of pin-makers. The young man's punctured carcass testified to an exit as hard as its journey had been easy. To the local chief inspector it would appear that the killer had perforated the lad's body with a blade like a letter-opener's.

At the time of this outrage Elsie was visiting Toledo, thrilling to El Greco's genius, including his *Martyrdom of Saint Sebastian* as well as to that city's wondrous filigreed swords, daggers, and letter-openers. Her incredulity, indeed, near shock, were unmistakable when the horrific news reached her. In panic, she rushed to Barcelona; once there, however, with remarkable composure, she made final arrangements —

the last of her travels with Lester. His porous remains she would escort
back to his appalled father, whose periodic subsidy, if already mailed,
would have to be designated "Return to Sender," since "Please Forward"
would be quite out of the question.

Monsignor Pouter presumably was the only living confidant who
knew of Astoria's early name change. With some compunction she
disclosed to him her "flirtation with vanity" while in Europe some years
before. This revelation was quietly divulged at a soirée, one of several
hosted by the prelate, who stoutly affirmed that "parties and penitents
were as complementary as scotch and soda." With ease this good father
could stir waves of remorse on the normally placid seas of his prodigals'
souls. One such ripple, as observed, ruffled Astoria, who mused that her
earlier life had been tainted with pride — a flaw which she felt her
recording angel dutifully noted.

A side benefit accrued to Pouter's unique apostolate. By overseeing
extirpation of guilt in others, he was spared from dwelling on any need
to rescue himself. In a word, this pastor had invested in a rewarding
brand of theology which larded him with consolation by doting on
others' aberrations, thereby muffling uneasy confrontation with closer,
personal mischief.

"Astoria," Elsie confessed, was chosen for an advantageous reason: it
recalled a town in her native Northwest, associated with John Jacob
Astor, patriarch of furs and fame. Her surname was another matter; its
origin had nothing to do with New York's lucrative "Meadows," but
owed its selection to her father's proclivity for poker. Early, she realized
any gambler considered a "flush" his winning hand. To hold an entire
suit spoke of power — no mediocre ambition in her estimation.

A leaden setting it was when Astoria Flushing stepped from Con-
course F and introduced herself to Lester's father, whose remorse over
his son's loss seemed oddly inconsistent with the prolonged and mutual
separation each had enjoyed for almost a decade. Brushing aside this
puzzle, Astoria appeared the soul of solicitude. The senior Ellison, a
widower, was struck by her sweetness and poise — sensations of softness,
he had believed, long buried with his wife.

The memorial Mass, a simple liturgy for a wandering son of the Church, was celebrated by the redoubtable Monsignor Pouter. When he finally intoned: "May the angels lead you into Paradise. May the martyrs greet you at your coming," Astoria, never tardy to seek out havens of security and pestered with the prospect of celestial deprivation, then and there determined to approach the priest for directions to what Dante enticingly describes as a realm of "unimperiled ravishment." Her incorporation into the "fullness of faith," as genial theologians call it, happened somewhat later, when baptismal water trickled across her tilted forehead, moistening a pearl earring which sparkled joyously for the occasion.

Burton Ellison, dredging up a courtliness which had slumbered following his wife's passing and his second marriage to Business, was not slow to insist that Astoria remain as his house guest, following the boy's interment, where, incidentally, Tad Rully uncharacteristically lingered over his task. Astoria eagerly accepted her host's invitation, and thus began a relationship which culminated in marriage, resembling, in many ways, the love of Tristan and Isolt; each party relished a mirage, a mute attraction at best, which flourished more in affectionate distance than union. It all ended, as the troubadours promised, in that inevitable and choicest separation, where passion really blossoms, namely, in death.

But prior to this grievous conclusion, Astoria, as a dutiful wife, ever protective and efficient, conferred on her spouse unstinting attention; he, in turn, experienced a happiness long presumed vagrant. She coaxed and mobilized his hopes, which, if not always realistic, were flattering. Even in business matters, the formerly imperious executive deferred to his darling's advice and schemes. All this gave associates pause. Eyebrows, like a Nikon shutter lens, blinked in begrudging admiration at the "Boss's Treasure," who, in four years, prospered in every sense, including that of beneficiary.

Time seemed to mellow and grant a generous reprieve to Ellison. His renewed vigor escaped no one's attention, including the "Gem of his Life," always doting by his side. What a shock then to read in the Monday morning *Monitor:* "Wealthy Executive Crushed in Bizarre Mishap." Though it took some time to sort through the tangle of details, a sorry picture emerged.

Astoria and Burton were relaxing over the weekend at their secluded country lodge, which, for weeks, had been groaning and fidgeting under extensive remodeling — all, of course, overseen by the "Lady of the House." Apparently, Ellison had retired to his den with its extensive library, the second cherished possession of his life. Detectives guessed that, as he reached for a volume of Gibbon's *Rise and Fall of the Roman Empire*, an entire section of shelving broke free of its hasp, tumbling thunderously upon him. The weight crushed him like a wafer. "One sprawling contusion," the coroner indelicately blurted to police.

When chaos had hushed and the heap was cleared, the corpse was found still clutching the last tome of Gibbon, as if some impish force orchestrated the symbolic finality of it all.

Astoria, who was upstairs at the time, rushed to the clamor; peering in, she found herself numb beyond belief, too paralyzed even to summon help for several minutes. No matter. Death pounced instantly. The culprit hasp, it was deduced, must have jarred loose in protest to all the hammering and sawing which had rocked the residence in recent weeks.

Thus it happened that Burton Ellison's young wife now became "The Lady," undisputed heiress of his fortune. Grief was assuaged by prosperity; remorse surrendered to resources. However, the prize would not remain uncontested for long. "No man is an Island," and an *Island* would prove the point.

Majorca, scholars insist, nurtured the soul of Spain's original inhabitants. These are the proud and close Catalan people, who stubbornly cling to their fertile language and culture against all odds to plant them into Spanish soil. Dispossessed of wealth and power, many manage to hold fast to a noble heritage, eager to vindicate honor when trivialized, or worse, exposed to ridicule.

Into this category fitted Ruiz Sanson Narvaez. He it was, as matters curdled, who penned a revealing letter in fractured English to a "Mr. Tad Rully." This note was posted shortly before a spider tumor mortally entangled Narvaez's faculties and dispatched him to Judgement. Ruiz wrote his message not to effect some kind of reconciliation with his Maker; rather, it served as a kind of radiation to combat another cancer, more virulent, which had invaded his heart and had been gnawing at its tissue for some time. With passion like Narvaez's in mind, *Ecclesiastes* cautions: "Laugh no man to scorn in the bitterness of his soul."

Any tourist knows that Majorca boasts of its "Hermitage," symbol of passions, where George Sand and Chopin consumed each other in requited love. A pity their fervor left frigid Elsie Madsen, who, earlier, like an ingenuous pilgrim, had visited this paradise. In her own grotto she was courted by Ruiz and seemed to repay his ardor with every favor short of marriage. "Impossible!" she shuddered. She was "another's property," brutally dominated by a degenerate, older escort, who terrorized her, stalked her like a plague, infecting her desire to live, let alone genuinely love.

The outraged, impulsive Catalan, as eager to revenge his lady love as to rescue her, concluded, incorrectly, that final liberation from her "tormentor" would emancipate the girl for him. Thus a permanent exit, at the hands of Ruiz Sanson Narvaez, awaited Lester Ellison, who must have expired with as much puzzlement as pain.

However, the victim's pain was not isolated; the Majorcan liberator too was soon sacrificed. Elsie, after her savior's heroics, crisply discarded him. The crime done, an obstacle removed, and a golden opportunity beckoning, Astoria Flushing skipped from Lester's itinerant world of subsidies to substance: namely, to their vulnerable benefactor, his father, whom she, over time, had heard and learned so much about. Astoria's gambit was bold and calculating, but like Washington's rugged coastline, not without shoals and an angry surf to threaten smooth passage.

Emulous of the Old World's love for its long past, the New World, more modestly, also hugs its briefer history. High school yearbooks abound, providing a link to time. If one were to peruse such a record preserved on the bookshelf of Tad Rully these twenty years, a salient

fact would emerge, scrawled across the face of a young man's provoca-
tively grinning picture: "All the best! To my only Friend! Lots of 'Lady
Luck' Forever! Les Ellison." Yes, the truant rich man's son and Tad, gift
to a barren mother, were, for those who tried to remember, inseparable,
even when distance played the spoiler. Occasional exchanges — familiar and warm — such as the one which Ruiz Narvaez ripped from his
dying victim's shirt, clearly testified to a genuine bond. Over time, with
Elsie's taunting repudiation always before him, the spurned hero
curiously culled, scanned, and memorized Tad's letter, until the now
cancer-wasted Majorcan felt as close to its sender as, in fact, was the
original recipient, his victim. A freakish sympathy surfaced in him, born
of a scalding revenge, which urged an alliance with the gravedigger,
ratified by a gift of rich information. It was this perversely pure token,
exposing the *real* lady and her treacherous ambition which was squeezed
into a "grieving" Astoria's hand at the gravesite, embellished only by a
phone number and modestly signed: "Theodore Rully."

To this day, bewildered townsfolk chatter in disbelief at the unlikely
marriage between the gravedigger and the heiress. Memory of the wedding Mass remains as fresh as were the autumn mums which winked
smartly from the main altar of Poor Souls' Church. Monsignor Pouter,
dipping into reservoirs of accommodation which must have taxed even
his limber conscience, gazed on the curious couple.

The ceremony seemed to illuminate the groom's face into something
seraphic. The portly celebrant favored a glance at the bride, who knelt
composed before him. Moved by her solemnity, he invoked the final
blessing.

Astoria, usually resilient, betrayed no radiant emotion during or
following the liturgy, only what was interpreted as reserved joy. "Not
improper," some reflected, "for one whose short life had known such
pain." But Elsie Madsen, a pragmatic believer in Moliere's dictum: "I

prefer an accommodating vice to an obstinate virtue," considered it tolerable to alter her name from "Flushing" to "Rully." "Astoria Rully," she sighed. "Perhaps . . . 'Flushing' was too much like a game of risk. Rully . . . Rully . . . Astoria Rully! It does have a ring to it not altogether inelegant."

Tad, for his part, grew quietly genial, with the unassuming smile of an Assisi among his swallows. Retired, obviously at peace with God and His world, he was regularly seen ensconced behind the wheel of his new Lincoln as it meandered lazily into the country setting of his former labors, Saint Calixtus' Cemetery. There, ritually, he would pause before one particular plot, nod, smile, and move on to the marbled presence of Saint Calixtus himself. For his ears alone, he would whisper a prayer of thanksgiving, grateful to have dug his last grave . . .

. . . .

NANCY BARTLEY: Nancy is a Seattle native. She holds a Master of Fine Arts in writing from the University of Washington, where she won the prestigious Loren D. Milliman Scholarship. Her short stories have appeared in literary journals nationwide. She also is a multi-award-winning journalist with a Pulitzer nomination for feature writing. She writes for *The Seattle Times*.

VICTOR BOBB: Victor, a native of Pullman, is an associate professor of English at Whitworth College. He has published more than fifty short stories and articles in magazines as varied as: *Modern Short Stories, Fundamentalist Journal, Emmy Magazine, Reason* and *True Romance*. He has played rugby since 1970, is a birdwatcher, is restoring a 1941 Chrysler, and lives north of Spokane with his wife and teenaged son and daughter.

KATIE BRADY: Katie is 30 years old and wrote this story under extreme duress for instructor Marilyn Smith of North Seattle Community College. She enjoys writing for recreation, but it just never occurred to her to submit anything for publication before. She has lived in Washington State for half her life, having grown up in a military family that moved frequently. She enjoys listening to punk and alternative music, playing with her cat and computer hobbying. Friends have described her as having an "acerbic wit."

MEGAN BREEN: Megan was born and raised in Spokane. Presently she is dividing her time between her own writing project and teaching others the creative process of fiction. She has been published in *The Wide Open Magazine* and *The New Renaissance*. Currently she is working on a novel about Spokane during the 1930s.

LISA COURTNEY: Lisa is a poet whose first book, *A Coming of Age*, was published in 1978. She is currently writing a novel and working on a collection of short stories. She lives in Seattle with her husband and two cats, one of whom is a rising star in the publishing industry.

JOAN DECLAIRE: Joan is an editor and feature writer for a Seattle-based health magazine. This is her first piece of published fiction. She has lived in Seattle for ten years.

DAVID A. DOWNING: David is 31 and a 1988 graduate of the University of Washington's Creative Writing Program. He won First Prize in the *Portland Oregonian/Northwest Magazine* 1988 Young Writers Fiction Contest, and shared the 1987 Louisa Kern Award. He works at the University Book Store, where he helped organize their Third Thursday Reading Series.

M. ELAYN HARVEY: Elayn is a native Washingtonian who lives in Enumclaw. She writes songs, poetry, articles, short stories, novellas and novels. Her work tends toward fantasy and science fiction. Her first science fiction novel, *Warhaven*, won second place in the Pacific Northwest Writer's Conference contest in 1986, and went on to be published by Franklin Watts in 1987. Elayn has delivered a trilogy to her agent and is currently writing a fantasy novel set in Enumclaw.

VALERIE LEAF: Valerie is 36 years old and happily settled in Seattle since 1984. She has an academic career spanning parts of three decades: University of Puget Sound and London University in the 70s; a science degree from U.C. Berkeley in the 80s. She is currently at work on a Master's Degree in Psychology with plans for a counseling practice. Current works in progress include numerous short stories, essays, and a longer, non-fiction project that chronicles the changing lives of women.

DON MASTERS: Don is a retired deck officer in the U.S. merchant marine. His hobbies are writing, reading and sailing his 25-foot sailboat. He is 68, married (twice), has two sons and a daughter and six grandchildren.

REBECCA D. WILKINSON NICKELL: Rebecca lives in Kent and has written for *Washington* magazine. She is currently developing a series of book projects; she works for Sasquatch Books in Seattle. An avid horse-woman, Rebecca divides her spare time between her horses and her new husband.

FATHER JAMES G. POWERS: Father Powers is a Jesuit priest. He is a professor of English literature and philology at Gonzaga University and is the Chairman of the English Department and Chairman of the University Board of Members. His specialty is 17th and 18th Century British Literature. His publications include: *A Cultivated Vocabulary* and *Handbook of Helpers; Amelia, Studies in Short Fiction, Human Development, The Bible Today*. His favorite authors are Henry Fielding, Walker Percy, Flannery O'Connor and P. D. James.

KIMBERLY M. REASON: Kimberly is presently the manager of a job training program for disabled adults. She will soon serve as Vice President of Programs at the Seattle Urban League. She volunteers as a speaker for the AIDS Prevention Network and People of Color Against AIDS Network (POCAAN), Vice-Chair of the United Way Youth Service Committee, Career Mentor for Campfire's Teen Parent Project, and is a project team member of Leadership Tomorrow.

DON ROBERTS: Don is a short-story writer working on a first novel. He was a second place winner in the recent Literary Lights competition. He has resided in Washington State for fourteen years. Don currently lives in Seattle with his wife and two daughters and is employed part-time at *Seattle Weekly*.

MARJORIE ROMMEL: Marjorie was born and raised in Auburn, Washington, where she lives with her husband and daughters. A journalist for 25 years, she operates Rommel Communications, a public relations and direct marketing firm, teaches part time at Highline College in Midway, and writes for and edits several area trade publications. She is a founding member of The Northwest Renaissance, a 16-year-old coalition of approximately 50 Puget Sound area poets. Her award-winning poems, nonfiction, essays and short stories have appeared in a wide variety of local, regional and national publications, including *Washington* magazine. She loves the rain.

JEANNE E. SCHULTZ: The Jeanne Schultz Suburban Training Camp for Family and Publishers operates year-round. During rewriting drills she recently completed a novel of Nez Perce Native history and adventures.

WENDY SLOTBOOM: This (*Rose Ann*) is the first short story Wendy has had published. She lives with her husband, Tom, in Ballard.

BETTY J. VICKERS: Betty teaches adult education and developmental English at Green River Community College, where she is also an editor of the faculty newsletter. She had been writing poetry and short fiction for more than twenty years, and her work has appeared in a number of regional and national literary magazines.